Last Chance Saloon

The Bethesda Falls stage is robbed and Ruth Monroe, the stage depot owner, is being coerced into selling up by local tycoon, Zachary Smith. Meanwhile Daniel McAlister returns from gold prospecting to wed Virginia, the saloon's wheel-of-fortune operator. Daniel hits a winning streak but is bushwhacked and has his winnings stolen.

Virginia sees this romance with Daniel as her last chance of happiness and no matter what, she's determined to stand by her man, ducking flying bullets if need be. Daniel and Virginia side with Ruth against Smith and his hired gunslingers.

Only a deadly showdown will end it, one way or another.

Last Chance Saloon

Ross Morton

A Black Horse Western

ROBERT HALE · LONDON

© Ross Morton 2008
First published in Great Britain 2008

ISBN 978-0-7090-8580-5

Robert Hale Limited
Clerkenwell House
Clerkenwell Green
London EC1R 0HT

www.halebooks.com

Typeset by
Derek Doyle & Associates, Shaw Heath
Printed and bound in Great Britain by
Antony Rowe Limited, Wiltshire

PROLOGUE

DAYLIGHT ROBBERY

When the stagecoach eased over the brow of the hard-packed road that ran between two massive boulders, the driver, Alfred Boddam, grinned. Mid-morning and, by God, they were almost two hours early. He gentled the four horses to a stop and applied the brake. One of the passengers enquired gruffly, 'Driver, why have we stopped?' But he paid him no mind. From the box he sat looking down over the wide lush valley, a hard callused hand rubbing his chin's bristles as he admired the view. Nestling on the east of Clearwater Creek was his destination, the town of Bethesda Falls. He chewed his lip, recalling his last visit. Miss Kitty Riley had taken a shine to him with her winsome smile and this time around he fancied pursuing that fine shapely figure of womanhood.

'Don't you worry none, folks,' he called down, 'we're way ahead of schedule!' They were early because their load was lighter; at the Guthrie Staging Post he'd dropped off shotgun rider Wally Egan, complaining over a bad gut.

Liked his food too much, that was Wally's problem.

Alfred reached for the brake lever.

'Let it be, driver,' said a muffled, slightly cracked voice to his left.

'Who in tarnation—?' Alfred turned in his seat and gasped.

Standing on the boulder was a heavily built man, his face mostly obscured by a dusty green bandanna, his eyes concealed in the shade from his brown hat's brim. He was pointing a revolver and the weapon shook to and fro, as if its owner was impatient. It don't pay to rile a man with a drawn gun, Alfred thought.

'Take it easy, fella. What d'you want?'

'Mr Boddam, sir, who're you talking to?' a passenger called out.

'Quiet!' the bandit ordered. Jerking his weapon at Alfred, he added, 'Throw down the strongbox and nobody gets hurt!'

'Now, hold on a minute, I—'

The pistol barked and red dust spurted around the hoofs of the rear horses. A woman inside shrieked, the horses whinnied and the wheel creaked as it strained against the brake shoe. 'Easy now, easy!' Alfred steadied the team with gentle movements on the reins. If only he could steady the passengers as simply.

'What was that?' a man snapped, whipping back the left-hand leather curtain. 'My God, it's a desperado – he's going to rob and kill us all!' Distressed murmuring came from inside.

Another bullet – this time splintering the woodwork of the coach, just inches from the window, forced the passenger to dart back into silence.

'Stay inside, dadblast you!' The bandit turned again to the driver.

Alfred had taken advantage of the distraction and grabbed the double-twelve shotgun which lay at his feet. He swung it round and aimed. But he wasn't fast enough. Two more shots rang out and Alfred coughed and sagged backwards, falling over the edge of the box and pinioning his body against the brake lever.

'Dadblasted fool!' snarled the bandit.

Inside the coach there were shouts and moans. A woman cried, 'Have mercy, sir!'

Ignoring the commotion, the bandit leapt from the boulder and landed noisily on the roof of the stagecoach. The woman and a man shouted in alarm. Edging past the driver, the bandit leaned inside the leather-covered front boot and heaved out the strongbox. He flung it to the ground. Then he checked the driver. His thick eyebrows raised in surprise. Only one bullet had pierced the reinsman's shoulder, the other must have missed; the old man had obviously hit his forehead and rendered himself unconscious: at least he was breathing.

'The old fool's lucky; he'll live!' he informed the passengers. 'Don't move, any of you!' he growled, and eased the unconscious man back on to the seat. There was nothing to wedge him in with. 'He'll have to take his chances, I guess,' he said, releasing the brake and jumping down to the ground. He landed firmly, despite his paunch, and whipped out his six-gun. Firing two more shots into the air, he slapped the hind-quarters of the nearest horse and the alarmed critters started moving down the slope towards Bethesda Falls.

Holstering his gun, the bandit ran across the road and picked up the strongbox. It was heavy and he carried it two-handed against his belly. Once he was behind the boulder, he threw the box down beside his patiently waiting roan. 'Steady, old girl,' he soothed.

He reloaded his six-gun. A well-placed bullet shattered the padlock.

Steadying his mount, he started stuffing the contents into his saddle-bags. Then he swung up into the saddle and rode round the boulder.

One last look down the trail then he veered off, heading south, a mite richer.

The downhill swaying motion of the coach dislodged Alfred Boddam and he fell forward, half into the front boot, his arm crooked over the side-lantern, hand dangling and bashing against the flapping leather curtain.

'What on earth's happening?' A passenger boldly peeled back the curtain and stared at Alfred's limp hand. 'Ohmigod! Mr Boddam's dead!' he shrieked. 'Nobody's driving our coach!'

CHAPTER 1

THE HOUSE ALWAYS WINS

When Daniel McAlister entered The Gem saloon, Virginia Simone's heart lurched against the fitted boned bodice of her red satin dress and she almost made a hash of triggering the concealed device under the roulette wheel.

Pulling her eyes away from the entrance with an effort, she turned back to her table and flicked the hidden lever to ensure that the house won. The ball bounced a few times and a couple of gamblers let out exclamations of surprise. But for Virginia it was no surprise at all. Yep, the house won when it mattered, when the stakes were high. She hated this part of her job, suckering the poor punters just to line the pockets of owners Royce O'Keefe and Zachary Smith. Still your foolish pride, she told herself; it's a job, and she was one of the best in the whole damned Dakota Territory.

'Better luck next time, gentlemen.' Leaning forward and offering the two players a generous view of her ivory skin set against the black fringe trim – the only compensation they'd get – she pulled the chips towards her with the croupier stick.

As if it was the most normal thing to do, though her pulse raced, she glanced up.

Daniel was limned against the bright rays of the sunshine streaming through the doorway, which he almost filled. He'd just handed over his gun rig to Mabel who was doing the ordnance check at the entrance. Now he was surveying the smoke-laden room as the batwing doors creaked behind him. The kerosene lamps suspended from the spokes of the ceiling wagon-wheel illuminated the room and Daniel. With a slight chill trailing her spine she noted that he had gained a long white scar from brow to cheekbone on the left.

Then he spotted her and approached, weaving past two waitresses in scanty skirts and revealing bodices. His eyes were not on them, but on her; they sparkled, the same deep grey-blue of the Missouri.

Her feelings about him were mixed, which wasn't so strange since she hadn't seen him in two years, and here he was sauntering in as if it was only yesterday.

As gentlemanly as ever, he whipped off his dusty white hat and grinned. She noticed that he was missing a tooth.

'Nice to see you, Miss Virginie.' His fringed boar suede shirt and buckskin trousers were trail-worn, stained and dust-covered. He could do with the mother of all baths, she reckoned, and would certainly benefit from a shave at Chauncey Wilcox's and some new scented soap that Mr Chapman had had delivered from Boston.

'Daniel,' she acknowledged. Then she eyed her two customers, both losers. 'Any more bets, gentlemen?'

'Nope, the wheel of luck ain't turning fer us, I guess,' said the gent wearing a moustache big enough to harbour rats. His companion grunted agreement and they rose from their stools and moved desultorily to the bar area.

As she watched them go, her heart sank. She recognized the big man at the bar, Saul Barchus, the brother of Mrs Monroe, and he was arguing with O'Keefe, which was never a good idea.

'Anything amiss, ma'am?' Daniel enquired, following her gaze.

'No, it's just Saul – he probably owes money he can't repay. Damned fool!'

'Well, a man has the right to throw away his money, don't he?'

'I suppose – if it's his to throw away.' She turned back to her table. As she automatically piled up her winnings, she observed, 'You look older, Daniel.' She reckoned that his two years' absence translated into about five in looks.

'Aye, well, ma'am, living in the mountains does that to a man. Loneliness wears him down and cuts time-lines into him.'

'Not to mention the odd wound,' she said, eyeing him with concern.

He touched the side of his face. 'Aye, this here scar was courtesy of a Sioux brave who didn't take kindly to my panning the stream.'

Another cold shiver ran down Virginia's spine. 'I take it you apprised him of his mistake?'

'Yes, ma'am, you *bet* I did!'

'Betting's what we do here. So, are you going to gamble tonight?'

'Sure. I thought I'd try my luck on the faro table. Don't rightly want to take no money off of a lady like yourself, Miss Virginie.' His cheeks reddened.

'It ain't my money; it belongs to the house – Messrs O'Keefe and Smith. If you play at my table, Daniel, the game will be fair.' It rarely was, but she could play fair if she had a mind and boss O'Keefe could go hang!

11

'You've always been fair in your dealings with me, even at Mrs Simpson's. . . .'

She was too wise in the ways of the world to blush, but she remembered with fondness their only night together, at Ma Simpson's bawdy house – Daniel honestly thought it was slang for boarding house, bless him, and she hadn't the heart to disillusion the great lummox. Ma Simpson's was on North Street, isolated at the far end, as if in quarantine; it actually faced the back lots of the El Dorado saloon and the Bella Union bordello. At least she hadn't had to find work there, even if by all accounts Grace Tabor ran a good clean parlour house.

Daniel agitatedly ran his fingers round the brim of his hat. 'I just want to increase my lucky strike.'

'So you finally made it!' She was genuinely pleased for him.

'Aye.' His look grew serious. 'And I'm a man of my word, Miss Virginie. I recall what I promised a while back. . . .'

A while? Two dad-blamed years! 'I know,' she said gently.

'I aim to double my money so I can keep that promise.'

She flushed at the prospect, trying not to recall what Daniel had said two years ago, making a promise she'd prayed that he'd keep. With a stern note in her voice, she said, 'The quickest way to double your money, Daniel, is to fold it over and put it back in your pocket.'

'I'm obliged for your concern, Miss Virginie,' he said, bowing slightly.

'Why don't you go and get rid of that trail dust instead?'

'Yeah, I've got so much dirt on me, I reckon I could sell myself off as real estate.' He smiled. 'I might do that, ma'am. I'd been meaning to have a bath and a shave before coming to see you, but I couldn't wait.'

Those words did strange things to her heart. 'I'm flattered. Go and wash – better than being taken to the cleaners here.'

'They have cleaning amenities in The Gem?' he enquired, glancing around.

Sometimes she wasn't sure when he was joshing; she waved him away, grinning. 'Go and get cleaned up at Mrs McCall's – she'll be pleased to see you, I'm sure.'

'I'll take your advice, ma'am,' he said and bowed. 'I'll be back later to double my money.' He donned his hat and moved to the checkout at the door.

A moment later, O'Keefe left Saul at the bar and strolled over.

As usual, Royce O'Keefe was in his deep-grey frock coat and fancy black and yellow vest which had two pockets, one to hold his fob, the other concealing an illicit derringer pistol. Beneath his sharp features and cleft chin nestled a silk puff tie secured with a jewelled pin. He thumbed at Daniel's retreating back. 'Haven't I seen that guy before?'

'Probably, Mr O'Keefe.' He had a good memory – especially for debt defaulters, she thought. 'He's been prospecting.'

He wafted a hand in front of his face. 'Yeah, smells like. Well, don't get too friendly with the punters – I've got waitresses for that. You just keep that wheel turning.'

'It's a quiet night, sir.'

'Yeah,' he agreed, biting off the end of a cheroot and spitting it onto the sawdust floor. 'Maybe we should've hired dancing girls from Paris, France, like they've done in San Francisco.' He lit up, dropped the lucifer and crunched his tooled boot heel on it. Through the blue-grey smoke he gave her a studied stare that cut her dead. 'Your looks ain't bringing in the marks no more, it seems to me.'

13

Before she could reply he turned away. Puffing a trail of smoke, he sauntered over to the faro game.

Fuming fit to blow steam out of her ears, Virginia gave a stiff welcoming smile to three cow-punchers who were strolling towards her table. She leaned forward, enticing and beckoning. 'Do you fine young men want a turn of the wheel with me?' That was not an offer they could refuse, particularly as none of them was young.

Daniel stepped out of The Gem saloon and was halfway across the main street when he heard a number of people shouting from the south end of town. A stagecoach was barrelling along past Zachary's Livery, the horses' eyes wide in alarm. Folk were scattering left and right to get out of harm's way.

'The stage – it's early!' exclaimed Saul Barchus, arms pushing aside the saloon doors. 'Hey, it ain't stopping at our depot!'

'It's driverless!' snapped Daniel.

'Oh, my God!'

Four distraught horses pulling more than a ton of coach bore down on Daniel.

CHAPTER 2

VERY BIBLICAL

Instead of jumping out of the way, Daniel ran towards the oncoming horses and leapt. Plain foolhardy, he reckoned, but he landed firmly on the central shaft, arms outstretched like a tightrope walker. His forward momentum and the opposite movement of the horses and stagecoach threatened to unbalance him and cast him down under the pounding hoofs and deadly wheels. Almost level with the tails of the lead horses, he grasped the harnesses with both hands and held tight. Jolted by the odd rut in the road, he barely managed to maintain his footing. Gathering up the dangling reins, he braced himself and then launched his body forward again, running the final length of the shaft's tongue. He sensed his left foot beginning to slip and jumped at the coach's front boot and grabbed hold of the metal rail of the driver's box. Grunting with the effort, he swung up and in and immediately started pulling back on the reins.

To his right he noticed that big fellow Saul running alongside the lead horse, straining his muscles as he attempted to slow down the animal, soothingly talking to it by name.

A few more yards and the coach had reduced speed sufficiently for Daniel to gently apply the brake. Then Daniel eased the unconscious driver back on to the seat. The man had lost some blood, but the wound didn't appear too serious. With Saul's help, Daniel lowered the driver to the hard-packed earth.

A slightly built male passenger bundled out, pulled off his glasses and wiped his sweating face with a handkerchief. He was followed by a heavy-jowelled individual with a lazy eye. Despite the leather curtains, their clothing was covered in a white patina of trail-dust.

'Horrendous!' Lazy Eye exclaimed. 'Absolutely horrendous!' He wore a well-used, slick-handled Buntline handgun in a tied-down rig.

'Who might you be?' Saul enquired.

'Randolph Slade, sir!' He waved a fist at Daniel, his blue grey eyes piercing. 'I'll be sending a telegraph to your company's director on the instant!'

Saul clapped a hand gently on Slade's shoulder and a small dusty cloud puffed up. 'He don't work for the stage company, Mr Slade.'

The passenger in glasses added, 'In fact, sir, he very likely saved our lives!'

'Oh,' Slade said.

'That's about the size of it,' Saul said, and eyed the little man.

'Horace Q. Marcy, sir!' He replaced his glasses and studied Daniel, his saviour.

Ignoring the two passengers, Daniel effortlessly hefted the wounded driver in his arms. 'I'll take him over to the doc's place.' He nodded at the shingle opposite. 'Mighty convenient, stopping here,' he observed with a grin. On the other side of the street was an attractive fenced house, complete with a cherry tree – Mrs Hiram McCall's Cherry

Tree Boarding-Rooms.

Saul laughed. 'You chose a mite dangerous way to hitch a ride, stranger!'

'Thanks for the help, Saul,' Daniel said, striding across to Doc Strang's.

'Hey, you know my name – what's your moniker?'

'Daniel,' he threw over his shoulder.

'Very Biblical, the pair of you!' laughed Carl Shull, the printer, who had hurried out of his shop. 'Might make an interesting article in the weekly newssheet.'

'I think you'll have enough to write about with the robbery an' all,' Saul remarked gruffly, as he helped the other four passengers down. 'You all right now, ma'am?' The woman nodded but seemed unable to articulate anything. Probably still a bit shaken. Saul glanced over his shoulder and breathed a sigh of relief. The Slade fellow wasn't heading for the telegraph office but lugging his carpetbag towards The Gem, where Zachary Smith seemed to be waiting for him on the boardwalk. The Marcy fellow was taking his bag to the hotel.

Saul said, 'If you folks want to freshen up at the hotel, I'll arrange for your bags to follow.' This offer met with murmurs of agreement and then, easing the horses round to head back to the depot at the other end of town, Saul added, 'Me, I've got to get these poor critters unharnessed, rubbed down and rested.'

Daniel had a rub down and rest too. Now his shirt and trousers betrayed the marks of a rigorous brushing. He wore a creased but clean buckskin jacket with deep pockets; it was long, reaching down to mid-thigh. His dark brown hair was almost black, plastered over his skull, and he'd had a shave. As he stood at the bars of The Gem's cash booth and bought $500 worth of chips, he apprehended his reflection in the ornate overhead mirror and reckoned he looked quite presentable, if he ignored the scar. Behind the teller was an enormous steel safe. On the right-hand counter were wads of bank notes and coins; coloured chips were stacked in wooden trays. On the left was a set of scales where prospectors' gold was cleaned and weighed and converted to money or chips.

Pocketing his chips, Daniel strode over to the roulette table.

He arrived during a break in the betting and Virginia glanced up. He liked it when she gave him that up-from-under look. Her coal-black eyes sparkled, mischievously, as if inviting him to say or do something daring. 'Howdy, Miss Virginie,' he said, 'I'm back.'

'So you are,' she replied, full cherry-wine lips smiling. 'And you sure are a fine specimen when you're spruced up, Daniel.'

He felt his massive chest swell at her words. 'Thank you kindly. Now I reckon I'll try my luck at the faro table.'

'Well, since you're determined to take a punt,' she said, 'I'll accompany you.'

'You will?'

'Sure, maybe I'll bring you some luck – though I reckon you've used up all your luck for one day playing at town hero!'

'Hero? Me?'

'Don't be so dadblamed modest,' she chided, fiery eyes full of admiration. 'The whole town knows you stopped that runaway coach.'

'I was lucky, I guess. And Saul helped.'

'Well, let's see if you're going to be lucky at cards, shall we?'

At that moment her relief, Mabel, stepped in by her side.

He nodded politely at Mabel, a slim blonde with an eye-catching *décolletage* that prompted him for decency's sake to move his gaze to the chuck-a-luck table.

Virginia gently touched his arm. 'Don't let Watt talk you into playing his game,' she warned him. 'The odds are too high.'

Mabel chuckled, her gold-tasselled ringlets shimmering. 'High ain't in it; the game came out West from England and its odds are a horrendous hundred and eighty to one. English robbers!'

'Stick to faro – the odds are nigh on evens,' Virginia said, as she checked her table's chips and money and signed off on a pad for her hour-long break. 'See you later, Mabel.'

Then she took Daniel's arm and his heart soared. 'Let's see if you've got any luck left, shall we?'

'You bet,' he croaked and they moved towards the faro table.

'Better food you'll be hard pressed to find out West,' opined Horace Q. Marcy, as he leaned against the bar of The Constitution Hotel.

Jack Berry, the bald proprietor, smiled smugly and tweaked his black moustache. 'I like to think so.'

'I can assure you, Mr Berry. Even Mr Lorenzo Delmonico himself would be honoured to partake of your cuisine. That brandywine beef was truly exceptional – the hint of cinnamon and Bourbon just right.' Marcy licked his lips at the recent taste-memory. 'I've travelled quite a bit, so my opinion is quite informed.' A hint of surprise coloured his tone. 'Aren't you concerned about the eatery that's opened up next door?'

'Not at all.' Berry grinned. 'I can stand a bit of competition – in fact, it keeps my chefs on their toes!'

'Yes, I can see that. Competition will make it possible for our nation to grow – it helps businesses thrive, doesn't it?'

'Say, Mr Marcy, if you don't mind me asking, how old are you?'

'Twenty-four this month. Why?'

'Well, you have a mighty old head on young shoulders.'

'I'll take that as a compliment.' Marcy gazed around as he sipped at his whiskey.

'I meant it, young man. Do you intend staying here long?'

'I was just passing through – but the stagecoach robbery has altered my priorities.'

'A bad business, that, sir. Pretty rare, robbery out here. You were unlucky, I guess.'

Marcy nodded. 'Well, by all accounts I was very lucky – my fellow passengers too!'

'Aye, that was a bold move that stranger made.'

'If we had a few men like him out West, the towns would be tamed in no time.'

'Oh, our town ain't so bad. It ain't wild, like some.' Perry dried a glass with his cloth. 'I heard the deputy's posse returning about an hour ago. They had no luck finding the bandit.' Berry moved away to serve another customer at the other end of the bar.

One foot resting on the brass rail, Marcy sipped his drink, deep in thought.

A swarthy man moved to the hotel bar and seemed purposefully to nudge Marcy with his elbow. Marcy's drink spilled on to the counter. He turned to the newcomer. The man was about his height, but much broader, with a lived-in face and bristles that could light a lucifer at ten paces.

'I reckon you owe me an apology, cowboy,' Marcy said.

'Is that so?'

'Now, Greg, there's no need to be causing a ruckus,' Berry said, moving towards them. 'I'll recharge the gentleman's glass. No harm done, eh?'

'That's as maybe, Jack, but nobody tells me to apologize!' Greg swung a fist at Marcy's astonished features.

But Marcy ducked swiftly enough to avoid the blow then took a step forward and straightened up, crashing the crown of his head under Greg's chin. 'Oh, terribly sorry, cowboy!' he said as Greg jerked backwards to the floor, unconscious.

As Marcy rubbed his head of thick hair, which hung long down to his earlobes, Jack Berry leaned over the counter and whistled. 'Well, I'll be—'

'An accident. What's the fellow's name again? Greg, was it?'

'Greg Bartlett. Works for Zachary Smith.'

'I'm sure he'll be right as rain in no time.' Marcy flung a couple of coins on the counter and retrieved his hat. 'Buy the man a drink when he comes round. It might help ease the pain in his jaw.'

'That's generous of you, Mr Marcy.'

'A cheap lesson in manners, I reckon. Goodnight, Mr Berry.' Marcy walked into the reception area and ascended the stairs to his room.

'Jeez!' he heard the co-owner exclaim. 'I wish I'd taken bets on that outcome!' Horace Q. Marcy smiled. Bethesda Falls promised to be quite interesting, after all.

The bets were small, five or ten dollars on each card number the players fancied on the layout. Suits were irrelevant.

Virginia whispered, 'Every so often O'Keefe lets the banker use a square dealing box.'

'Square?'

'It ain't gaffed.'

'You mean Mr O'Keefe cheats us customers?'

'Hush,' she hissed, looking around, but nobody was paying them any attention. 'Do you want me to lose my job?'

'No, of course not, Miss Virginie. But it don't seem fair, if the house can cheat.'

'That's the way the business works. The odds favour the house anyway. But O'Keefe likes an edge to pay for his fine clothes and home, you know.'

'What would happen if he was exposed as a cheat? I know I'd be mad as a peeled rattler.'

'He'd be either horse-whipped or lynched. Depends on the mood of the men, I suppose.' She hesitated, peering up at him. 'You're not thinking of saying something, are you?'

'No, though if I had hard evidence on him, I'd likely take it to the sheriff.'

'Just play the cards, Daniel.' She nodded in the direction of the faro banker. 'Tonight you're really in luck – Reggie has a square box.'

Reggie Connolly was a short man with long grey whiskers. He wore a green visor to shield his eyes from distractions and the overhead lights. 'Place your bets, gentlemen,' he intoned.

Daniel put two five-dollar chips on the four and the same stake on the nine. A new gambler sat next to Daniel and bet on the six and the queen. Then it was time for the banker to deal.

With a smooth practised action, Reggie first pulled the losing card out of the box and placed it on the right – a six. The next card was put down on the left of the box; this was the winning card – a four; Daniel gained twenty dollars. Reggie claimed the newcomer's stake for the bank. On the side of the table opposite the banker was the case-keeper, who kept track of the numbers revealed: the banker's bowler-hatted sidekick flicked a four and a six on the abacus-like apparatus. Everybody could see how many of each number had been played.

Next time round, Daniel put a ten dollar stake on the queen, leaving his earlier bet of ten on the nine as well.

Several players groaned as Reggie pulled out a doublet – the losing and winning cards were fives. The banker took half of the stake on the five. As Virginia explained, that was the only edge the house had – in a fair game.

Before long, Daniel had amassed considerable winnings. Virginia gripped his arm tightly, excitedly. 'You need to stop soon, Daniel,' she whispered. 'Your luck can't hold much longer.'

He patted her hand. 'With you on my arm, Miss Virginie, I reckon my luck is the best in the world.'

'Smooth talker,' she whispered.

'OK, folks, who wants to bet the turn,' Reggie enquired.

Only three cards were left in the dealing box. A swift check of the case-keeper revealed that the king, ace and four were left.

Daniel put down fifteen dollars, betting the order they'd come out would be four, ace and king.

He guessed right and won sixty dollars, since the bet offered a four-to-one payout.

'It must be your lucky night, sir,' Reggie said, expertly unwrapping and inserting a fresh pack of cards into the dealing box.

'It seems so,' Daniel replied.

Virginia squeezed his arm. 'Well, take care. My hour's up. I need to get back to my wheel, else Mr O'Keefe will get real disgruntled.' She patted his hand and glided away.

He hated to see her go but he decided that he'd

continue playing until he lost a quarter of his winnings. That would still mean he was up on his stake by seventy-five per cent.

At one point Daniel put ten coppers – six-sided tokens – on the eight, effectively reversing the action and betting that the eight would lose. 'Inspired play, sir,' Reggie said, as the eight did indeed come up on the right side of the dealing box – a loser for the other players yet a winner for Daniel.

He grinned and pocketed his winnings. 'I reckon I've taken enough off you, sir,' Daniel said, gently.

Reggie nodded and smiled. 'I know you have, sir. Well done.' He turned to the other players. 'Maybe your luck will change, gentlemen,' and took more bets as Daniel moved away.

Using his knuckle to nudge his flat white hat away from his brow, Daniel could hardly believe his luck. Grinning broadly, he strode through the batwings and stepped down from the boardwalk.

Crossing Main Street diagonally, he patted his bulging buckskin jacket pockets, and stepped up to Chapman and Riley's General Store. Among items of a more practical nature, such as claw-hammers and scythes, the window display presented a selection of ladies' bonnets. Daniel fancied buying one tomorrow for Miss Virginie. Maybe the blue, since he reckoned it would complement her auburn hair, which he guessed was long though he'd only ever seen it banded and gathered in ringlets. But he didn't know her size. Well, she was small compared to him, but he didn't want her to be disappointed if he got the wrong fit.

He stepped down, a loose puncheon board creaking, and made his way across the entrance to First Street West, which was really only an alley with a grand name. The street lamp on the brick corner of the bank cast light and created long shadows. But shadows didn't concern Daniel one bit.

A mewing sound alerted him. Unmistakably, it was an animal in distress. He glanced left, into the shadowy alley-way. On the right was a barred side door to the Hayes Bank; on the left, a cluster of crates, doubtless from the general store.

It was definitely a cat. Sure, he'd killed his fair share of wildlife – including cougars – but he couldn't abide seeing a creature in pain. And the cat, wherever it was, seemed in serious trouble.

Daniel moved into the alley. He only covered a few paces before he saw the poor tortoiseshell thing. Its right forepaw had been recently severed, its stump still bleed-ing. A short length of rope secured its neck to the bottom of a drainpipe that ran down from the gutter of the store to a soakaway drain.

'Here, kitty, kitty, who's done this terrible thing to you?' he asked gently, kneeling down in front of it. He reached out to unfasten the rope.

Defiant to the end, the cat hissed and slashed at him with its remaining fore-paw, claws extended.

Daniel jerked back and, though he was quick, he didn't avoid a slight scratch on the back of his right hand. 'You ungrateful little squirt—'

'We could say that about you, *monsieur*.' The booming, slightly foreign-sounding voice emerged from the dark-ness a little further down the alley.

Nobody of an honest disposition should be lurking down here among the shadows, Daniel reasoned. Slowly, licking his scratched hand, he unwound his powerful frame to its full height, hand hovering close to his holstered Army Colt. 'I reckon you picked the wrong man to rob, mister,' Daniel said.

The blow on the back of his head was so powerful it would have crushed the majority of human skulls.

Dry-gulched!

He caught the heady sweet aroma of some kind of perfume and abruptly felt his knees pound into the hard clay earth. Without being able to stop himself, he slumped on to his right side, where he lay next to the cat. His cheekbone hit the ground, but even now he was not completely unconscious. The metallic taste of blood was in his mouth. His head pounded and his vision was hazy, as if he was looking through some thin gauze-like material. And all of his considerable strength seemed to have deserted his limbs. Barely eighteen inches away were the boots of one of his attackers. Elegant tooled boots. Maybe he was going to end up in boot hill, he thought. Despite the ringing in his ears, he picked up two voices.

'You weren't supposed to brain the *imbécile*!' That booming voice again.

'Why not?' His cowardly assailant, with a tobacco-roughened tone. 'Might as well shoot the sucker.' A six-gun was cocked, very close to Daniel's ear. He didn't flinch. His body wasn't too enthusiastic about responding to his wishes right now. He felt like hell and it looked like he was going there real soon.

'Put that gun away, *espèce d'idiot*!' snarled Booming Voice, moving closer. 'Most of these marks will gamble again and we can rob 'em blind more'n once!'

The hammer was lowered and the gun rasped as it entered its holster. 'Ah, yep, now that sounds good.' Tobacco Voice's breath stank as he leaned over Daniel and moved his hands through the buckskin jacket pockets and found the bundles of notes, his winnings. 'Jackpot!'

'*Parfait*! Let's go before the law does his rounds!'

'You ain't afeared of Jonas, are you?'

'There ain't much I'm scared of, Frank, but I don't invite trouble.'

The cat howled.

'Can I put that critter out of its misery now?' wheedled Frank.

'No, gunfire will bring with it witnesses.'

'Chris'sakes, you're a real killjoy!'

'That's enough, Frank. I've got another chore and it promises to be good sport for the both of us. . . .'

'You mean, a woman?'

'*Précisément.*'

Daniel heard nothing else as he blacked out then.

CHAPTER 3

WOLF SLAYER

It was past midnight when Virginia left the saloon and crossed Main Street. She'd have liked to call on Daniel, but Mrs McCall didn't take kindly to womenfolk visiting her male boarders at any time of day, let alone this late. She'd wait until the morning, perhaps catch him then. Word had spread through the saloon about 'the hero's luck' and she wanted to congratulate him on getting his winnings.

She stepped up on to the boardwalk at the front of Hayes Bank.

Suddenly she heard something, a noise like a fearfully sick animal. For an instant she debated about the advisability of going to investigate. No matter, she couldn't leave one of God's creatures in pain.

At least the street lamp reduced the alleyway's shadows to a sombre gloom.

She saw the cat and her heart overturned. It hissed at her but its actions were weak, half-hearted. The poor thing had probably lost a lot of blood. Yet it persisted in licking the bloody stump. The cat hadn't made that pain-filled sound, though.

Unravelling a shawl, she wrapped it round the animal.

It struggled a little then seemed to accept the sweet cloying scent and warmth offered.

She started as she heard a groaning noise, near the general store's wooden crates.

Abandoning the cat, she stood up and walked tentatively towards the sound, her throat suddenly very dry, her heart pounding.

She glimpsed the huge bulk of a man and hesitated. Now would be a good time to rouse the deputy sheriff. Then her heart fluttered as she recognized him. 'Daniel!' She held up her skirts and ran.

Kneeling by his side, she noticed the blood on his head. 'Daniel!'

He groaned again. 'Oh, Miss Virginie, I'm so sorry.'

'Sorry?' She wiped a trickle of blood from his mouth. 'Whoever did this should be sorry!'

'They took all my winnings.'

Her stomach churned and her heart lurched. 'That's terrible!' She guessed who was responsible, but without proof, Sheriff Latimer or Deputy Jonas couldn't do a thing. It wasn't the first time a winner at O'Keefe's tables had been bushwhacked.

'Now I'm poor as a hind-tit calf! I'll have to go and find me another stake before I can come back and wed you!'

Her heart went out to him. Until this moment, she had tried to be cold to his return, fearing he'd have changed – and he had, after all – fearing he wouldn't wish to remember his rash promise after a single night of passion two years gone. But Daniel McAlister was a man of his word and indeed that was one of the many things she loved about him.

'Never you mind about any stake, you big ox. Don't you know I'd marry you even if you were stony broke?'

'You would, I mean, you will?'

'You name the day and I'll railroad the preacher!'

'Ouch,' he groaned, lifting a hand to his jaw, 'I guess I won't be laughing for a while. Though I'm laughing inside now and I reckon I won't stop till the day I die.'

'Hey, stop getting maudlin on me! Let's get you to Doc Strang.'

Using Virginia for support, Daniel struggled to his feet. 'Nothing feels broke. But I hurt something awful.'

'Not as much as someone else will before the week's out,' she assured him.

Daniel looked at her askance.

'Never mind,' she said, 'let's get you to the doctor.'

He stopped in his tracks. 'No, wait, the cat – maybe the sawbones can help. . . .' He walked giddily over to the drainpipe and knelt beside the bundle of shawl. Inside, the cat was asleep, its chest gently rising and falling. Daniel unsheathed his knife and carefully cut the rope and lifted the bundle to his chest. The cat purred and its single front paw extended its claws and plucked at his boar-skin shirt.

Virginia wiped her eyes with a handkerchief, mindful that her make-up was slightly smudged.

Dabbing smudges of dust from her freckled rosy cheeks, Ruth Monroe surprised herself and spent time studying her reflection in the mirror. She soaked the flannel from the queensware washbowl and ran its welcome cooling surface at the back of her neck and over her high fore-head and around her wide light blue eyes. The lines at the corners of her eyes suggested that she was older than thirty-five. 'You're a fine-looking woman.' That's what Dillon had said, God rest the kindly soul. She'd been a widow for seven years and she was aghast to realize that she felt an itch, an itch to enjoy a man's company again. This land either kills off women in childbirth or widows them because of the rampant violence.

She detected moisture in her eyes and it hadn't come from the cloth. No, she wasn't mourning her husband. Now, at this moment, she was brought up by the realization that no man was likely to look at her in the way Dillon had. She'd been eighteen when the horse kicked her in the face. They said she was lucky only to get away with a broken front tooth and a thick scar running down from her nostrils across her plump lips. Ever after, when she smiled, it turned out more like a grimace. 'Have no fear, those lips kiss real fine,' Dillon had consoled her afterwards.

God, she missed his kisses, his strong embrace!

Her breasts pushed against the white cotton camisole as she gulped a great breath and then sighed.

Ruth dropped the cloth in the bowl and put her hands on hips, arching her back. What I'd give for a long soak in the tub, she thought. But that was a luxury she only managed once a week, on Sunday afternoons. Most times, she was in the office working on the books or helping out in the corral, like today. Her shoulders ached at the memory.

'This isn't a civilized time to call, Drinkwater!' That was her brother Saul's resonant voice.

Moving to the window that overlooked the stagecoach depot's entrance, she squinted through the slightly warped glass pane.

Carey Drinkwater was standing outside with his sidekick Frank Gordon. Ruth felt her cheeks flush with anger. She pulled on a robe and hastily tied its belt. Grabbing the bedside lantern, she descended the back stairs to the office.

'Saul,' she called, 'what's going on?'

Silhouettes were in the doorway, standing on the board-walk.

'Sis, it's—'

'Ah, Widow Monroe!' exclaimed Drinkwater, never missing a chance to remind her of her loss. 'Stay with the

monkey, Frank, while I talk to the organ-grinder!'
Drinkwater was burly with square shoulders. He barged
past her brother, which was no mean feat as Saul was big-
boned, large as a bull. But he was a gentle giant and
Drinkwater knew that only too well.

Legs quivering under the robe, she straightened her
aching back and glowered. 'Couldn't your "talk" wait till
morning?'

Fingering his swallowtail beard and moustache,
Drinkwater acted as though he was considering her words.
Then, withdrawing a wad of banknotes from inside his
jacket, he tossed it from hand to hand. The dry line of a
mouth opened. 'Mr O'Keefe is willing to be generous,
ma'am.'

'What's that you're toying with, Mr Drinkwater?'

'This, ma'am, is something *supplémentaire* I'm entitled
to give you over and above the original offer. It needn't
appear in the sale transaction documents.'

'Why do you persist with the phoney French words?
They don't fool me!'

Ignoring her remark, he added, 'A business induce-
ment.'

'A bribe, I think it's called.'

The lantern flickered on his gimlet eyes and cratered
complexion. 'I'm not one to bandy about with words,
ma'am. Do I tell Mr O'Keefe that you're going to recon-
sider? It would make my day to take him such good news.'

'You can tell your boss whatever you like, Mr
Drinkwater. But I am not selling – to him – or to anybody
else, for that matter.'

Drinkwater shrugged and put the money back inside
his jacket. He grinned, showing crooked teeth. Turning
on the heel of expensive French hand-tooled boots, he
passed Saul at the door. He stopped for a second and

swiftly pulled out his Colt .44, slashing its barrel savagely against her brother's face, the ramrod opening a long bloody gash from brow to cheekbone.

Ruth let out a yell and almost dropped the lantern.

Saul backed into the desk and groaned, a hand rising to his bleeding face.

'Now *that* made my day,' Drinkwater said. Stepping outside, he added, his voice booming, 'Wait till you get my *encore*!'

In the shadows across the street, Randy Slade turned to his boss, Zachary Smith. 'That fancy dude's got no idea. She won't give in to bribes.'

Smith cracked his knuckles and nodded. 'That's my opinion as well.'

Slade's piercing grey eyes glinted as he withdrew his Navy Buntline .44 revolver and twirled the cylinder. 'Do you want me to chase her out of town?'

His pallid complexion going even paler, Smith shook his head. 'I don't want any shooting – leastways, not yet. I have plans for that place – and the town, come to that. I don't want a shot-up stage depot.' He cracked his knuckles again. 'No, we'll bide our time and wait for the others to turn up.'

'Maybe the man you're waiting for will be on the next stage?'

'I hope so. I've only got rumours to go on, of course. A friend of a friend at their headquarters says their man is coming through here on reconnoitre.'

'I reckon nobody on my stage fitted the bill.'

Fingering his long slender beard, Smith smiled. 'Let's see what my partner does next.'

'You need that gash looking at!' Ruth said firmly, shoving

her reluctant brother ahead of her up the steps leading to the doctor's surgery.

'Stop fussing, Sis! It'll heal of its own accord.'

'Stuff and nonsense! D'you want to look like me?' The backs of her hands batted him harder than she ought.

'Hey, Sis, go easy!' He glanced back at her. 'There ain't nothing wrong with you,' he told her, 'if you set your mind to getting a man.'

'Fiddlesticks! This isn't about me – now get in there!' she barked, as he opened the door.

She made to follow Saul inside but bumped into him. He'd stopped moving and stood half-inside the doorway. Somebody else was already in the surgery waiting room. 'Ma'am,' Saul said, nodding.

'Mr Barchus.'

Ruth peered round her big brother. 'Do I know you?' she asked the overdressed hussy. What was that bundled in her shawl – a baby?

'It's Miss Simone,' Saul said, 'from The Gem.'

'So it is,' Ruth said sourly. 'Go on, get inside, man.' She pushed her brother in and closed the door.

The bundle meowed and Ruth's demeanour softened a little.

'Are you next with the doc, ma'am?' Saul asked.

Virginia shook her head. 'No, I brung in a friend.'

'I didn't know Will Strang did vet work,' Ruth observed.

Virginia smiled. 'Oh, this is a stray we rescued. No, my friend's in the surgery now – though he insisted the doc sewed up this little mite's wound first. Doc says it ain't any different to a human, to fix a wound.'

'I suppose not,' Ruth allowed.

'Is your friend all right, Miss Simone?' Saul asked.

'I reckon. He's pretty darn tough. He was bushwhacked and robbed.'

34

'Well,' Ruth said, 'you'd know all about robbing folk blind, wouldn't you?'

Virginia raised an eyebrow. 'I beg your pardon, Mrs Monroe?'

'Fleecing my brother, that's what!'

'Now, Ruth, there's no need to go talking like that!' Saul turned to Virginia. 'Mr O'Keefe was reasonable tonight; he said he'd wait till the end of the week for his money.'

'*End of the week*!' Ruth exclaimed. 'How much do you owe?' she demanded.

Saul didn't get a chance to answer. At that moment, the surgery door opened and Daniel lumbered out; just behind him, the bleary-eyed Dr Strang was wiping his hands on a towel.

'Daniel!' Saul exclaimed and grabbed his sister's arm. 'This is the man I told you about. He saved the stage and our passengers.'

'I'm obliged, sir,' Ruth said, giving him a nod. 'That was very brave of you.'

Daniel grinned; now he had two teeth missing.

Ruth faced Dr Strang. 'How is Alfred, Doc?'

'He's recuperating in the spare room above the general store.' Strang winked. 'It seems he and Miss Kitty have a liking for each other. . . .'

'Oh . . . well, I'm pleased he's going to be all right.'

'That's a nasty cut there,' Daniel said, squinting at Saul. 'Sorry I kept you waiting.'

'It's nothing,' said Saul. 'I'm sorry about your bein' bushwhacked in our town. 'Specially after what you done.'

'It's a bad business.' Dr Strang sighed. 'See he reports the attack to Deputy Johnson in the morning, Miss Simone.'

'Yes, I will, Doc.' She fished in her reticule. 'How much do I owe?'

35

'I've settled already. Our resourceful Mr McAlister had a special little pocket the brigands knew nothing about.' The doctor held up a coin then wagged his finger. 'And make sure he rests for a day or two. Don't take a "no" from Widow McCall, you hear?'

Daniel groaned. 'Two days in bed!' He shook his head.

'You should be so lucky, mister,' Ruth said, massaging her back, then turned to Dr Strang. 'Can you take a look at Saul? Carey Drinkwater pistol-whipped him.'

'He did, did he?'

'Yep,' said Saul.

'And I don't suppose you'll prosecute?'

Ruth shrugged. 'What's the use? The Frenchified swine will have so many witnesses saying he was elsewheres, it'd be a waste of time.'

'Frenchified?' Daniel queried.

'Yes, the fool throws in the odd French word. Supposed to hark from New Orleans, but I ain't so sure.'

'Does he wear some kind of perfume?'

'Yes.' Ruth wafted a hand, as if getting rid of an unwelcome smell. 'A mite overpowering. Eau-de-Cologne, he calls it. From Paris, France.'

'Then I reckon he was one of the two varmints who bushwhacked me.'

Virginia laid a hand on his arm. 'I'll get the deputy to call in on you tomorrow. Now come on, let's get you back to Mrs McCall's before you're locked out!'

'I hope she kept some of that pie back like she promised, I'm starving,' he replied.

Virginia laughed. 'Good night, Doc, and thanks!' She helped Daniel to the door. 'And Mrs Monroe,' she said over her shoulder, 'watch out for that Drinkwater critter, he's a mean bastard.'

'Er, yes, thank you . . . I will.'

36

Deputy Jonas Johnson licked his short pencil and scrawled a few notes in his small writing-pad while Daniel and Virginia watched. Daniel felt self-conscious, lying in bed, propped up by several pillows.

'Right,' said Jonas. 'I'll pass on your report to Mayor Pringle. He'll know what to do. The circuit judge is due in six weeks.'

Standing at the bedside, Virginia said, 'Aren't you going to arrest Carey Drinkwater, then?'

'Well, he has witnesses says he was somewheres else.'

She stamped her foot. 'I suppose one of them is Frank Gordon, is it?'

'Well, yes, it is – how'd you know that?'

She laughed emptily and turned to gaze at Daniel.

Daniel said, 'The guy I reckon was Drinkwater spoke to his accomplice, called him "Frank". I put that in my report, Deputy.'

Jonas shrugged. 'So you did. But Gordon has witnesses who place him in a poker game at Ma Simpson's.' He slid his writing pad and pencil into his shirt pocket.

Sighing heavily, Virginia said, 'It's no use, Daniel. O'Keefe and Smith have the town sewn up—'

'Hey, Miss Simone, there's no call to use that bad talk!' Jonas snapped. 'Sheriff'll be mighty displeased at them aspersions.'

'Maybe,' she said. 'What do I care?'

Jonas strode across the room, opened the door and slammed it behind him. The sash window rattled.

She smiled and leaned over Daniel, kissing him lightly on the lips. 'I thought he'd never go!'

He breathed in the heady scent of her and wanted the kiss to go on but she straightened up. 'You minx!' he exclaimed. 'You riled Jonas on purpose to get rid of him!'

'You bet!'

Absently putting a hand in her skirt pocket, she withdrew a set of three shells and a pea. 'I keep these, my old standby. They help pass the time.'

'Aye, and make you a few dollars as well, I shouldn't wonder.'

'Fancy your luck, mister?'

'What're the stakes, ma'am?'

'A kiss.'

'You mean, if I win?'

'Yes,' she said.

'What if you win, ma'am?'

She smiled, lips glistening. 'Oh, I'll settle for two kisses, I reckon.'

Virginia was adept at the shell game and Daniel never once guessed correctly under which shell the elusive pea was hiding. If this was losing, he wasn't complaining.

After a while, she pocketed the pieces and brushed a hand over his features and ran a finger down his scar. 'Does that still hurt some?'

'Nope.' He smiled. 'I kinda like you doing that, Miss Virginie.'

'Kissing?'

He nodded, grinning. 'And touching . . .'

Disappointingly, she lowered her hands demurely to her lap. 'Maybe one day you'll tell me about it – the scar, I mean.'

'Maybe I will,' he said, remembering.

It was back-breaking work, sifting through the stream bed with his tin wash pan, but Daniel had persisted. There was no way he would return to Bethesda Falls or anywhere else civilized until he'd found his fortune. The trading post supplied all his needs and ran a catalogue service for rare or fancy items. He'd cope. Somehow.

His theory was that over time any gold residue from underground watercourses would wash downstream and swirl and congregate in pockets of material that was least disturbed by the rushing water. That was near the base of stones and boulders. As a theory, it might be hopeless, but he gave it a try. He was only too aware that gold in its native state was dull unornamental stuff; only false gold presented ostentatious glitter. And before long, he was finding particles of lacklustre yet genuine gold just where he expected.

Every day, for hours on end, he scooped sand and dirt from around submerged rocks and filled the wash pan. That was the easy part. Then he'd swirl it around just under the water, an almost mesmerizing circular motion, relieved by the odd jerk in and out of the water so that the lighter material would wash away, leaving only the gold-carrying residue. He kept at it until his arms and hands were numb then continued a little longer.

He was into his second week when he had an unwelcome visitor.

'You steal yellow metal from my people's stream!' The stern voice came from behind, in the bushes by a cluster of rocks and pine. Daniel recognized the Lakota language, a haunting musical sound, even when the speaker's tone, as now, was stained with anger.

Hastily dropping the wash pan, Daniel grabbed for the Henry repeater rifle that rested close by on a flat stone. But a moccasin-covered foot stepped on the stock, preventing him from lifting it.

As he slowly unwound and stood up in the stream, Daniel expected to feel an arrow piercing his vitals or a tomahawk slicing into his chest or skull.

The moccasin belonged to a tall, powerfully built Indian. The feathers and trappings declared he was Sioux. His nose was hooked, his dark eyes flashing out of the shadow of deep brows – the lineaments of a proud man. Muscles well toned, the Sioux warrior regarded Daniel with disdain. 'You and your kind steal our land, destroy our way of life. You threaten our sacred places.'

'I didn't think your people went in for possessing the land,' Daniel replied, in halting Lakota.

'*Paha Sapa* is sacred! Your tone rebukes Wolf Slayer!' the Sioux barked.

'Grimm Mountain ain't in the Black Hills, fella, so it ain't sacred by my reckoning!'

'Despoiler!' Swiftly picking up the rifle, the Sioux flung it into the bushes.

'Hey, that cost me forty-five bucks!'

'Everything is money to you white men!' snarled Wolf Slayer as, knife drawn, he sprang off the rock.

Stumbling back and to the side, Daniel avoided the slashing knife. But he slipped on a mossy stone. Hitting his pelvis painfully against a submerged rock, he rolled away, towards the far bank, frantically fumbling for his sheathed hunting knife.

Wading through the stream, Wolf Slayer came after him.

Daniel got to one knee, withdrew his knife and splashed water at the oncoming Indian's face. As the Sioux warrior was deflected for a moment, Daniel sprang.

He grasped hold of the wrist of the Indian's knife-hand and twisted harshly but the blade didn't drop. Wolf Slayer grabbed Daniel's wrist and simultaneously brought up a knee, thrusting it into Daniel's belly. Daniel gasped, falling backwards, yet he managed to hold on to the Indian's wrist and Wolf Slayer fell on top of him. The man's breath was

40

foul, but he imagined his own wasn't much better.

The underwater rocks were smooth but unforgivingly hard against his back. Spluttering, stream water lapping round his face, Daniel felt his strength ebbing as Wolf Slayer thrust a knee on his chest, pressing down hard. It wouldn't take long before his rib-cage broke under the pressure. Wolf Slayer's free hand was clamped around Daniel's throat, trying to force his head under water.

Gasping for breath under the throttling hold, Daniel reached out with his left hand and lifted up a large rough stone and slammed it hard into Wolf Slayer's lower back. The vicious blow was surprisingly effective, as if it had ruptured some internal organs, and dislodged the Sioux sideways.

Surging with all his strength, Daniel broke free and heaved himself out of the water, slashing left and right with his knife. He heaved in air, but a moment later Wolf Slayer grabbed Daniel's wrist and was on top of him again.

They grappled bodily, rolling in and under the gushing water, now struggling along a small tributary.

Wolf Slayer's knife slashed down Daniel's face and the cut was agonizing; for a frightening second Daniel feared that he couldn't see as blood filled his vision. Blindly pummelling with a fist and slashing with his knife, Daniel finally rose to a standing position. Gulping in air, fighting down the pain from bruises and that nasty cut, he wiped the blood from his eyes, prepared to fight or, more probably, die.

But the threat was gone. Not two feet away, Wolf Slayer was sprawled in the tributary, his torso partly on a boulder, his legs submerged. The Indian's own knife was lodged in his stomach and the water around him was discoloured.

Through narrowed eyes Wolf Slayer glared at Daniel, hands batting at something in front of his face. 'You are finished,' the native said, 'I see you are like a wraith already.'

41

The wound was fatal, Daniel knew, and clearly Wolf Slayer was dying, his vision fading.

Sheathing his knife, he strode over to the Indian, leaned down and lifted him in his arms. 'You haven't got much time, Wolf Slayer,' Daniel told him.

The man's words came out as a faint whisper: 'What will you do with me?'

'I will honour you, as befits a brave warrior.'

Gently laying the Indian down on the dry earth, Daniel rested the man's back against the trunk of a ponderosa pine. Wolf Slayer winced and the fingers of his right hand wrapped around the hilt of his knife. He nodded, as if realizing for the first time that his life was ending.

Daniel stood up and stepped back. 'If you have enough wind, I reckon you better start your death song.'

Wolf Slayer's face twisted as he pulled the blade free, but he made no sound to acknowledge the pain. He nodded. 'Let it be so.'

Birds stopped singing and it was as if the very breeze stilled in the sparse treetops. Wolf Slayer sang and a chill ran up Daniel's spine and he felt light-headed, so tragic yet moving were the dying man's words. Facing death. Not fearing it. Simply acknowledging it.

Unseen amid the undergrowth a pair of grey eyes watched.

Afterwards, Daniel climbed the mountainside and spent three hours chopping down and splicing pine trees. Finally, he returned to Wolf Slayer's body and carried his dead adversary over his shoulder, up the mountain, to the burial platform he had constructed. Shakily climbing the makeshift ladder, Daniel lowered Wolf Slayer onto his last resting place. Clambering back down, he destroyed the ladder and gave the dead warrior a perfunctory salute.

42

CHAPTER 4

CHANCE

On the next day, Daniel found the stone he'd used to strike at the site of Wolf Slayer's kidneys; lodged in its side was a good-sized nugget of gold. Soon afterwards, he found substantial gold deposits in the stream, not far from the place where Wolf Slayer had been mortally wounded. If he'd allowed himself to be chased off, he'd still be broke. But instead, he realized, he could go courting! First, though, he must build a house. And he decided that he needed to conceal his discovery from claim jumpers – and other Indians. He was here at this place of death and great riches for the long haul, which amounted to almost two years.

'Two years I've waited for you,' Virginia said, standing at the foot of his bed. Her hands were in front of her, clasping an embroidered cloth bag. 'I reckon I can wait a mite longer, though I'd dearly love to snuggle in there with you right now!'

'Miss Virginie!' Daniel exclaimed. But he was smiling.

Her attractive face turned serious. 'Are you fit to get up tomorrow?'

'You bet. Why?'

'Because you're going to return to The Gem and win your money back, that's why!'

'I don't have the stake money any more, Miss Virginie. I'll need to work on my claim for a few more months, I reckon—'

'No, you won't. You must use my money as the stake.' She loosened the pretty draw-string and opened her bag.

He held up a hand. 'No, Miss Virginie, I won't take your money. I aim to keep you with my own honest toil.'

'When we're married, that'll be just fine by me. For now, you need my money for the game. And stop calling me Miss Virginie: plain old Virginia will do.'

'Sure, Virginia. Though I don't reckon you're either plain or old.'

She giggled. 'That's better. Now, I promised you we'd win back your stolen money, and I too keep my promises.'

'You're taking a great chance.'

'So did you, Daniel, prospecting for gold so you could wed me.'

'I found gold; I found you: I think we'll now have a chance of happiness.'

She grinned. 'Chance has nothing to do with it,' she said.

'Chancing your arm, aren't you?' Sheriff Latimer said, shifting his backside on the mattress. He felt the blood drain from his face, as every movement was still agonizing. The damned red long-johns didn't help, either; he'd much prefer lying in the buff. For now, though, he was presentable in his undershirt. He'd even shaved in bed – and been alarmed at how wan his normally sun-browned complexion had become since he was confined here.

His wife Lauri, her silver-grey hair tied in a tight bun,

fussed over the pillows, plumping them, her thin lips betraying annoyance at this intrusion.

Virginia shook her head. 'Only a little, Sheriff. I know how the game works. All I'm concerned about is that your deputy will be there. To see fair play.'

'Fair play?' Latimer gave a snaggle-toothed smile.

Virginia pouted. 'Daniel only wants to get back what was wrongfully stole from him!'

Latimer ran a hand through his grey hair then nodded. 'I'll have a word with Jonas.' He laughed and this time it hurt and he coughed. 'Damn and blast!' he seethed.

'Henry, you've got to rest!'

'Yes, all right, Lauri dear,' he said. Then he grinned at Virginia. 'I'd like to be there, Miss Simone, I really would!'

'Well, you can't!' Lauri said firmly. Turning to Virginia, her eyes a sparkling hazel, she added, her tone good-humoured, 'I think you'd better go, lass. I'm thinking you're a corrupting influence on my husband.'

Virginia smiled. 'No, ma'am – your husband's incorruptible and our town's lucky still to have him.'

'That's sweet of you to say so,' Lauri said.

Latimer growled, 'When you've finished talking about me, can you leave me in peace, eh? Like the doctor ordered!'

'Requested, dear,' Lauri countered as Virginia made for the door. 'The doctor *requests* his patients to do his bidding; only grouchy sheriffs order people about.'

'Your telegram's been sent, sir, as requested,' Cecil Kent, the telegraphist, informed Wally Egan.

'Thanks.' Wally turned and almost bumped into Horace Marcy entering the telegraph office. 'Sorry, mister—' His thick eyebrows shot up. 'Hey, dadblast it, weren't you one of our passengers?'

'Yes, Mr Egan.' Marcy stepped aside to let Wally pass.

'I just got into town this afternoon.' He removed his hat briefly to scratch his unruly curling brown hair. 'I couldn't believe it when Mrs Monroe told me what happened.'

'Yes, it was quite distressing.'

'Dadblasted varmint!' Wally thrust out his dimpled pointed chin. 'Deputy Johnson reckons he got clean away.'

'So I understand. How's your disability now?'

'Disability?'

'Your troublesome stomach?'

'Oh, that!' Wally beamed. 'I'm just fine now.' He winked, his face close to Marcy's. 'I just had to be near the out-house for a few hours, if you know what I mean?'

Assailed by Wally's foul breath, Marcy backed off a little. 'Of course. I'm pleased that you've recovered. It's a bad business, the robbery, isn't it?'

Wally nodded. 'It is that, mister. If only I'd been there—'

'Yes, most unfortunate timing, Mr Egan.'

'Well, I'm going over to the doctor's now to see how Alf's getting on. Then I'll mosey on to that eatery, see if Mrs Cassidy's special is still as good as last time I was here.' He rubbed his stomach and gave a half-hearted wave. 'See you around, mister.' He left.

Turning to Marcy, Cecil said, 'Howdy, sir. What can I do for you?'

Marcy peered at the blank writing pad on the counter. 'I'd like to send a telegram.'

'That's what I'm here for, sir.'

'Yes, of course.' He pulled off the top sheet from the pad, pocketed it then began to write. 'It's to my San Francisco office. Here's the wording.' When he'd finished writing, he tore the sheet off and passed it over.

Cecil read it through and raised an eyebrow.

'I know your discretion is total, Mr Kent,' Marcy said, and to emphasize the importance of the communication, he removed the blank sheet from the top of the pad and pocketed that too. 'And I appreciate that.'

'Discretion is my middle name, Mr Marcy. I'll send it right away.'

'Thank you,' Marcy said. Money changed hands. 'I'll call in tomorrow to see if there's been a reply.'

It wasn't long past dawn on the following day when Daniel got out of bed. Mrs McCall expressed concern as he entered her dining room for breakfast. When he ignored her pleas, she finally shrugged her shoulders. 'One of these days,' she said, 'I'll come across a man who ain't stubborn.'

'Yeah,' Daniel replied, 'but I bet he'll be real boring!'

A tear welled in her eye. 'You're right there, Mr McAlister. My poor Hiram was a stubborn old fool, but he was never boring.'

'I'm going to pop over to see how Mr Boddam's getting on,' Daniel explained. 'An invalid's gathering, you know?'

'You do whatever you like, Mr McAlister. You've earned the privilege, by all accounts.'

The general store was busy and Miss Riley flushed in front of several customers when Daniel asked about Alfred.

'Oh, he's upstairs.' Flustered, she glanced at her elderly business partner, Spence Chapman.

'Go on, take the man up, lass!' Mr Chapman said, shooing her away. A couple of customers chuckled.

'Follow me, Mr McAlister,' she said, and led Daniel past the counter into a back room and then up a flight of stairs.

On the landing, she stopped outside a door and knocked.

'Who is it?'

47

'It's Miss Riley, Mr Boddam! I've got *another* visitor for you.'

'Well, show the visitor in, please.'

Miss Riley opened the door and let Daniel in and closed it after him.

'I've dropped by to see if you're feeling any better,' Daniel said.

The stagecoach driver shifted in his bed and beckoned. 'Come over here, fella. Let me thank you for what you did.' He indicated a big-boned man sitting on a chair at the bed-head. 'This is Wally Egan, my shotgun rider – when he ain't skiving off with gut-rot.'

'I'm sorry about that, Alf. I told you. I—'

'Pay me no never mind, son. This here's the man who stopped the coach. Maybe saved my life!'

Wally stood up and offered his hand. 'An honour, sir.'

'Daniel McAlister.'

They shook.

'Well, I'd better be going, Alf. After I've eaten, I've got a dadblasted report to write.' He nodded at Daniel. 'Seems I may not have a job as shotgun no more. Head Office ain't too pleased with me.'

'It'll blow over, you'll see,' Alf commiserated as Wally got to the door.

'Yeah, let's hope so. Pleased to meet you, Mr McAlister. And thanks for saving my pard here.' He shut the door after him.

'How are you coping, anyway?' Daniel asked.

Alfred chuckled. 'If I'd known this would get the attentions of a fine woman like Miss Kitty, I'd've got shot long ago!'

Daniel nodded at the bedside table cluttered with fruit, bars of chocolate and a couple of James Fennimore Cooper books. 'At least you've got no shortage of stores.'

48

'Aye, but no alcohol, dadblast it! Kitty doesn't appreciate the curative powers of the stuff, that's the problem.'

Daniel laughed. 'I'll bring over a bottle, when the
coast's clear. OK?'

'You really are a life-saver, Daniel McAlister.'

Daniel entered The Gem and made a bee-line for the
roulette table. 'I've got the last of my stake money,
ma'am,' he said loudly. 'I'd like to chance my luck with
your wheel of fortune.'

Virginia smiled. 'That's sporting of you, sir. How much
do you want to wager?'

Slowly, in sight of the milling crowd, Daniel pulled out
$1700 in small denomination bills.

Her heart did strange things in her rib-cage as she saw
her hard-earned savings lying on the green baize table.

Deputy Sheriff Johnson, the only man allowed to carry
a gun in the saloon, came over and escorted Daniel to the
cash booth where money was exchanged for chips.

Time after time, as rehearsed yesterday in his bedroom,
Daniel won. However, to give the impression of a fair
game, he lost twice, but his stakes then were small.

A crowd gathered – among them the heavy-jowelled
Randolph Slade and tall humourless Zachary Smith. The
tension mounted.

So far, Virginia had managed with her under-table
contraption to steer the roulette wheel to favour Daniel.

Finally, O'Keefe strode up to her table. 'Miss Simone,
I'll take over now.' In response to a suspicious murmur
from the massed onlookers, he added, 'Gentlemen, I must
ensure the house plays fair.'

Ignoring the dubious mumbling, Virginia shrugged her
attractive bare shoulders, as if it was of no consequence to
her. Surreptitiously, she flicked the switch and, taking a

step back, she relinquished the table.

Standing beside the sheriff and behind O'Keefe, she tried to watch without showing any concern, her palms clammy and her mouth dry.

She'd already rigged the device so that when her boss took over, as she had surely known he would, him flicking the switch would do exactly what *she* wanted.

O'Keefe thought he was weighting the wheel-spin in his favour when he was actually ensuring that Daniel won one last time.

Just as he spun the wheel, O'Keefe whispered in her ear, 'The house always wins in the end, you know.'

Not this time, she thought, hearing the familiar faint clicking sound as O'Keefe manipulated the roulette device.

Deputy Sheriff Johnson escorted Daniel out through The Gem's batwing doors. On either side of them clustered a number of cheering punters.

'The hero wins again!' someone called.

'I got him to rub against my arm for luck!'

'And this time the deputy's making sure he don't get robbed!'

At the back of the room, resting his knuckles on the green baize tabletop, O'Keefe scowled. Eventually, he straightened up and his right hand fingered his vest pocket, where the derringer nestled. Swearing harshly, he turned on his heel and strode into the back office.

Outside, a buckboard with two horses was waiting at the hitching rail; Daniel's chestnut was tied to a cleat at the rear. A single lantern illuminated the boardwalk, the steps and the wagon. In the back of the buckboard, a tarp covered something large, like a trunk.

Main Street was sporadically lit on either side; mellow light spilled out from a number of windows belonging to the dwellings above the various shops. The Constitution Hotel was busy, light splashing onto the dusty hardpan.

Daniel clambered aboard, took the reins and bent down to shake Jonas Johnson's hand. 'Thanks for arranging this, Deputy.'

'No problem, Mr McAlister.' Then, leaning closer, he added in a whisper, 'She's waiting in the El Dorado alley.'

Daniel nodded. 'Thanks.' He geed up the horses and rode down the main street, his jacket pockets bulging with more money than he'd ever possessed in his life. His heart was hammering too, though not because of the riches he possessed.

Opposite the blacksmith's he turned right, into an alley. The El Dorado was noisy, the piano sounding slightly off-tune.

Virginia stepped out of the shadows, a bulging carpetbag in one hand. She was wearing a round crowned hat, its small curved brim decorated with a rooster feather, and it matched her dark green dress with gigot sleeves. The lantern on the corner of the boardwalk highlighted her face as she looked up, her thin eyebrow arching. 'Going our way, sir?' she enquired.

'Our?' he queried.

She turned slightly. In the crook of her left arm was a bundle which meowed once but didn't move. 'I heard you take in waifs and strays, sir.'

'I sure do, ma'am,' he said, raising his hat, and jumped down.

He relieved her of the bag and took her hand. She swung a leg up, the edge of her dress falling back to reveal black ankle boots.

By the time Virginia settled on the seat beside Daniel, the cat was fast asleep.

While the vast majority of the town slept, Deputy Johnson strolled the two blocks from The Gem to Monroe's Stage Depot. A figure emerged from the shadows, a 12-gauge double barrelled shotgun in his hand. 'Howdy, Elliott, it's me, Jonas.'

Elliott Quincy stepped into the lamplight. 'Everything OK?'

'Yeah, I was just seeing off a mighty lucky couple—'

'I heard. Well, if you're here now because you're thinking of tilting your hat at Mrs Monroe, you'd better speak up. She ain't getting any younger.'

Jonas flushed. 'How'd you know I'd taken a shine to her?'

Elliott grinned. 'You forget, I'm married – and have Beth, a lovely little girl.' He shook his head. 'But I wouldn't want to go through all that sparking again.'

'All what?'

'Courting! Will she like me, will she marry me? Endless questions and worries.' He turned, soberly. 'Besides which, I reckon Mrs Monroe's too old for you anyway.'

'Oh, is that so? I'll have you know I'm twenty-three in September.'

'Yeah, Jonas, that's old.'

Jonas chuckled and glanced up and down the street. It was quiet, just how he liked it. Mayor Pringle seemed amenable to swearing in two temporary deputies to stand watch over the Monroe depot. It seemed a mite overcautious, but if the mayor reckoned he had the funds in the kitty, who was he to object? He rolled a quirly; Elliott declined. Lighting it, he stepped down from the boardwalk. 'Well, I'll leave you to it. Mike Carney will be here at midnight.'

'OK, boss,' Elliott Quincy said.

Jonas quite liked the sound of that. Boss. Yeah. He kinda liked that.

'You wanted to see us, boss?' Drinkwater said, closing the office door. Gordon made his way to a high-backed chair while Drinkwater slumped into a settee. O'Keefe occupied one imposing desk to the left; another remained empty on the right, its name-plaque announcing: *Mr Zachary Smith*.

O'Keefe leaned back in his chair and lit a cheroot. 'Did you see that at the roulette table?'

'Yeah, boss. I reckon the guy's crazy as a loon. There's no way he can hold on to that kinda money.'

At that moment the door opened and Zachary Smith entered, dragging Mabel with him. He was tall, over six two, rugged, with big square shoulders; he towered over the hapless woman.

'Royce, she has something to tell you.' Smith was in his late forties but looked as though he'd already met his Maker, his complexion was so pallid. His dark eyes were fierce, gunmetal in colour. He stood, thumbing his tawny stiletto beard.

Shaking her head, Mabel looked away, her eyes puffy with crying.

'Mabel, you *do* have something to say, isn't that right?' Smith ground out the words between clenched teeth then raised his hand to slap her.

She flinched and took a faltering step away from him. 'Yes,' she whispered hoarsely.

'Well, spit it out, woman!' snapped O'Keefe.

'Virginia cleaned out her room . . .' she said, her eyes moving from O'Keefe to Smith. 'She was going to join the hero – tonight's big winner—' Mabel shrieked as Smith hit her anyway. She slumped to the carpeted floor, half-leaning against O'Keefe's desk, crying without making a sound.

O'Keefe glared down at Mabel with distaste, then the features of his face seemed to freeze as he turned to Drinkwater. 'Bring my money back,' he said, his voice cold and emotionless. 'Every last cent.'

Slowly unfolding from the settee, Drinkwater nodded. 'It'll be my pleasure, *monsieur*.' He jerked his head at Gordon to follow him.

The door slammed on the pair and Mabel started at the sound and looked up fearfully at O'Keefe, but both men seemed to have forgotten her presence.

'What's the news on the Monroe depot?' Zachary Smith asked, walking around his desk. Adjusting his grey frock coat, he sat down.

'Drinkwater delivered a generous offer. Silly bitch refused.'

Smith rested his feet on the leather-framed blotter. 'I don't want to sound impatient, but time's passing – we don't have much of it left.'

'I know, Zack, I know. I'll collar the fellow as soon as he comes into town. He was supposed to be on this week's stage. But your pal Slade says he didn't show. When he turns up, I need to delay him somehow till Monroe decides to sell.'

'Why's she going to do that?' An edge of impatience crept into his voice. 'What's going to change her stubborn mind?'

'Don't know. But I'll think of something.'

'I'm surprised she's coping as it is. Can't you use her brother's debts as leverage?'

'I'd hoped to, but the fool only gambles so much. She keeps his finances on a short leash.'

Smith laughed. 'Poor fool. It ain't as if he gets any

recompense off of her for abiding by her wishes!'

'Recompense?'

'Of the carnal kind, I meant.'

Mabel gasped at this suggestion.

'Hell,' Smith exclaimed, 'I forgot she was still there!' He rushed up out of his chair.

Mabel cowered against O'Keefe's desk.

'Did you hear what we were saying?' Smith demanded. He cracked his knuckles and she flinched. She nodded then shook her head, her eyes full of tears, lips quivering.

'Leave her be, Zack. She knows where her loyalty lies.'

Smith grabbed Mabel's arm and pulled her to her feet. 'Git, afore I get real ornery! Or is that horny?' He laughed as she fumbled with the door, exited and left it swinging.

Walking over to the door, Smith said, 'I've been thinking.'

'About what?'

'The Monroe woman. She can't cope by herself; she needs her brother. Without him, she'll give in.'

'That's entirely possible,' O'Keefe agreed.

'I'll look into it,' Smith said, and went out and shut it after him.

O'Keefe stared, wondering what his partner had in mind.

CHAPTER 5

DEATH STARING UP

Their buckboard had travelled a fair distance before Daniel said, 'I think we're being followed.'

'You're sure?'

He shrugged. 'Can't be, at this time of night. Just now and then I've caught a glimmer of moonlight on dust behind us.'

'What will you do?'

Without replying, Daniel steered the two horses to his right, down a rugged track amidst several ponderosa pines. He stopped the team and applied the brake.

'Let's wait and see.' Daniel pulled out his revolver and loaded the sixth chamber. 'Keep down in the back,' he urged her.

They waited. Even the slightest sound that the horses and their bridles made seemed deafening, blatant signposts to their hiding place. Then the horses' hoof-beats grew louder, closer. Daniel cocked his revolver. Two men rode past and Virginia stifled a gasp of recognition.

Once the sound of the riders diminished, Daniel said, 'You recognized them?'

'Yes. It was Drinkwater. I'd know his fancy clothes

anywhere. I reckon Frank Gordon was with him.'

'I guess they think I'm an easy mark. Drinkwater said he'd rob us winners blind more than once, if he had the chance.'

'Drinkwater's just hired help. It's O'Keefe – he wants what he thinks is his money. . . .'

Daniel sighed.

'It's pride with him.'

'Aye, but we didn't "win" any more than he stole from me in that alley!'

'That's true, dear, but it cuts no ice with O'Keefe – or his henchmen. They won't ever forgive you for winning it back.'

'Well,' he said grimly, 'let's make it a little more difficult for them, shall we?' Daniel urged the team forward. A couple of miles down the trail it branched off, one road leading to the Judd ranch, while the other was a circuitous route to Grimm Mountain. 'It won't be the most comfortable ride, but I can get to my place from here,' he said. 'Are you happy to stick with me, Virginia?'

She hugged his arm. 'Happy? Don't be silly, Daniel. I'm jubilant!'

'And here's me thinking you were called Virginia, Miss Jubilant.'

Playfully smacking his massive bicep, she laughed. 'Drive on, my man!'

According to the depot clock, it was just gone eleven when Elliott spotted a woman hurrying across the street. She wore a fancy frilly red dress – something he'd like his wife Annie to wear but she'd simply scowl and call it common. Feeling a little foolish, Elliott raised his shotgun and cocked the weapon. 'Steady, ma'am. That's far enough.' He glanced left and right but there was nobody else about.

This woman wasn't some kind of distraction, then, though he had to admit that her attractive appearance distracted his eyes. 'State your business, ma'am. It's kinda late for visitors.'

'My name's Erica Beal and I've come to see Mr Barchus. Saul Barchus.'

The upstairs sash window was opened and Elliott peered up. 'Sorry to disturb you, Mrs Monroe, but this lady—'

'That's no lady!' Ruth said.

Erica stamped her foot and raised her voice. 'This lady's going to have your brother's child, so I'd thank you to keep a civil tongue in your head, Widow Monroe!'

The window slammed shut.

'Are you going to shoot me, Elliott Quincy?' Stepping forward, Erica barged past him. 'Me and my unborn child?' She stood at the door to the depot and, arms folded, flung over her shoulder, 'I thought not.'

The door opened. Holding a lamp, Ruth stood in her robe, her blue eyes piercing. 'What's this nonsense you're spouting to half the town?'

'It's no business of yours,' Erica countered.

'Why'd you come here with your lies?'

'It ain't lies! Go see Doc Strang – he'll tell you!'

Ruth laughed hollowly. 'What – tell me that Saul's the father? I don't think so!'

'I'm with child and – and—' She pointed past Ruth. 'And he's the father!'

Swirling, Ruth faced her brother. The colour drained from her face as she saw the distraught look in Saul's bloodshot dark grey eyes. His dour mouth was downturned.

'He paid for a half-hour of my company every Saturday night!' Erica exclaimed.

58

'I thought you were throwing away money on gambling,' Ruth said, 'not this . . . this. . . .'

Saul's face crumpled. He lowered his head, averting his eyes. 'I paid for Erica's favours a couple of times,' he mumbled, 'but that's her job. She ain't supposed to get with child.'

Pivoting round, Ruth slapped Erica on the cheek. 'Go away, you harlot!'

Erica put a hand up to her face and glanced pleadingly at Saul but he wasn't looking at her.

Ruth signalled to Elliott. 'I'll have this deputy escort you from my premises if you don't go!'

'All right, I'm going!' Erica sobbed and stumbled across the street, hunched up, hugging her woes to herself.

As Ruth watched the girl leave, she said, her back to her brother, 'Go inside, Saul. We'll talk tomorrow.'

'OK, Ruth.'

Letting out a deep sigh, Ruth said, 'I'm sorry you witnessed that, Elliott. Can I get you a piece of pie or some coffee?'

He tipped a finger at his hat brim. 'No, thanks, ma'am. My Annie'll have supper waiting.'

Ruth nodded. 'That's good. I envy you – a doting wife, a young daughter.' She swallowed.

'Yeah, my pal Reuben says the same: I'm a lucky guy.'

'Sorry,' she said awkwardly, moving to the door.

'Jonas, the deputy, he feels—'

'Please don't mention any of this to Mr Johnson or anyone else. I'm sure it'll be round town soon enough, but I'd like to speak to my brother first.'

'No problem, ma'am. My relief, Mike Carney should be here in twenty minutes.'

'Thank you. I appreciate what you're doing. Goodnight, Elliott.'

*

The buckboard bounced uphill, over rugged tracks and small rocks, one horse stumbling slightly. At least the full moon afforded them adequate light so that Daniel could avoid treacherous ruts and boulders.

'Actually,' Daniel said, consolingly, 'we'll get to my modest cabin a few hours early by going this way.'

Virginia laughed. 'Just as well – I'll need the extra time to tend my bruises!'

'I've got liniment for that,' he offered and, though she couldn't quite discern his features in the half-darkness, she reckoned he was grinning.

She snuggled up to him. 'Never did organize that preacher, did I?'

'Nope,' he said, 'though I don't think that's going to stand in our way, do you?'

A while further along the trail, Drinkwater pulled in his horse and Gordon stopped alongside him. Drinkwater pointed. The earth here was soft, loamy.

'I don't see any fresh wagon tracks,' Drinkwater snarled, turning back in the saddle. 'They've taken the Judd road, damn and blast them!'

'You reckon they're going over the mountain?'

'Oh, yes. That's where they reckon the gold is and, let's not forget, the lucky swine had plenty!'

'Who reckon?' Gordon wanted to know.

'The Grimm brothers.'

Gordon chuckled. 'That's a fairy-tale!'

'Stop jawing,' Drinkwater snapped, his tone tinged with menace. 'O'Keefe isn't going to be too pleased if we go back without his money!'

*

Ten minutes after returning to bed, Ruth couldn't settle. Suddenly the night erupted with shouting and gunfire. She jumped out of bed and peered through her window.

Elliott stumbled into view, staggered a couple of paces and crumpled on to his knees. As her heart somersaulted, she detected a shadowy movement across the street, behind a horse-trough in front of the new restaurant with its quaint hoarding, 'Eatery'. Then the shadow had gone, melting into the darkness.

Tears streaming down her cheeks, she flung on her robe and hurried on to the landing. She knocked on Saul's door twice then opened it. 'Saul, did you hear—?'

Saul wasn't there; his bed hadn't been slept in.

Although she felt her legs wobble and all she wanted to do was collapse on the nearest bed, she found inner strength from some place deep within her and grabbed Saul's lantern.

Making her way downstairs, she rushed through the office and unbolted the door.

A couple of men were approaching hesitantly.

Carrying the lantern with her, she ran down the steps and across the hard earth to the ominously still shape. She lowered the lamp to the ground and, oblivious of her aching muscles, she turned Elliott over.

Ruth sobbed, recognizing death staring up at her.

The wagon moved over smooth stone and the horses' hoofs echoed. Moonlight revealed a clearing and ahead was a dark shape that seemed to rear up in front of them. Grimm Mountain. Somewhere quite near – to her left, Virginia reckoned – there was the constant rush of flowing water.

Daniel applied the brake and descended from the buckboard. 'I hadn't intended bringing you here just yet.

Be patient while I set the lights.'

She nodded.

He smiled then left her, melting into the deeper darkness ahead.

Perhaps she should have been anxious, sitting there, but she wasn't. Her pulse raced. This was a big turning point in her life, she knew, but she was going to relish it. She stroked the cat and felt quite calm. Gradually, the darkness lifted. Windows – with glass in them! – spilled honey-coloured light onto the wooden veranda and walls. On the right was a rough-hewn lean-to that served as an airy barn.

Virginia gave a start as Daniel appeared by her side at the wagon. She hadn't heard his approach, despite him wearing boots and the ground being rock.

'It's only a miner's shack,' he said, 'but for a long time I've hoped that you'd call it home.'

She swallowed, unable to reply.

He helped her down then abruptly swept her up into his arms. 'May I carry you over the threshold?'

'You're a mite premature, Daniel McAlister.' He laughed and was about to lower her to the ground when she added hastily, 'But I'd like it just fine. We can talk about a preacher tomorrow.'

Carrying her with ease, he crossed the veranda, teased the door open with a foot and moved inside, mindful of the narrowness and managing to avoid banging her head on the jamb.

'My humble abode,' he said, lowering her to the smooth split-log floor.

She held his hand and smiled. 'It's a lovely cabin.'

'Built it all myself, these last two years.'

The hewn log walls were bare. A table stood in the middle of the room, capable of seating four, with rough-cut chairs to match. A kerosene lantern dangled from a ceiling beam and another flickered in the middle of the table. In the right-hand corner was a huge wooden chest with metal bands round it. There was a window on both sides of the door. She decided that the place could do with a woman's touch – curtains on the windows, a table cloth, and maybe even a wall tapestry or two.

'Take a look,' he urged, letting go of her.

She walked across the room, running a hand over the table top, where she lowered the shawl-covered cat; its nose twitched but it continued to sleep.

On the left was a stone fireplace and hearth, and against the wall a dresser with a half-dozen plates displayed. In the corner was a white porcelain washbasin. An animal rug was spread in front of the hearth and suspended over the fire was a black pot. 'It gets hot in here in the summer, 'specially when I cook up something.'

She nodded. 'I can imagine.' She cocked her head to one side. 'What's that? It sounds like running water.'

Daniel crossed to the fireside rug and peeled it back; underneath was a hatch door cut into the floor. He knelt down, gripped the countersunk metal ring-handle and lifted the trap-door. 'Just like those fine dwellings in Boston and New York, this home has fresh running water!' About three feet below, a down-flowing stream gushed.

'I can pan for gold without being seen,' he explained.

'This is absolutely amazing!'

'And,' he added hastily, 'I might add that the out-house has a different watercourse.'

Virginia smiled. 'Yes, that's much more hygienic.'

She continued her perusal. Cow hide hung over the doorway which led into the back; here, a coal-oil lamp flickered, revealing a single bedroom with a window. A large padlocked wooden chest stood at the foot of the crude wooden double bed. On the left was a tall mahogany wardrobe and on the right a plank door.

He leaned against the bedroom doorpost. 'There's a lavatory out back, if you want to go?'

'No, I'm fine, thanks.'

'I'll settle the horses then bring in your trunk while you make yourself comfortable.' He left her and stepped outside.

Yes, it needed a woman's touch, no doubt about it. A bit primitive, but liveable. She ran a hand over the carved patterns on the kitchen dresser. He had spent a lot of hard-earned money on furniture that should appeal to an appreciative woman. He was so damned thoughtful!

Whenever she made what could amount to a life-changing decision, she harboured niggling doubts. But not this time. Here, now, it seemed right. Nary a doubt entered her head. She smiled at that realization just as Daniel came in with her trunk.

'You seem pleased,' he said.

'I am. I'm just happy to be here, Daniel. Here with you.'

'I'm glad.' He lowered the trunk and pushed it next to the wooden chest in the corner. 'I'll leave it here for now. Tomorrow, you can unpack. I've got spare wardrobe space in the bedroom.' He flushed. 'Tomorrow will do, won't it?'

'Tomorrow will be just fine, Daniel.'

'Hungry?' he asked.

She nodded, wondering if he was referring to food.

'I'll make a meal – just so you know I'm not marrying you to make you my household slave.'

Unpinning her hat, she took it off. 'I should hope not. Thanks.'

He relieved her of the hat and coat and hung them on a peg next to the cow hide door-flap. 'I'm sure you can thank me later, if you have a mind to,' he said.

'Perhaps I can,' she whispered, her eyes ranging up and down his body as he unbuckled his gunbelt and hung it on the back of a chair.

'I'm real sorry to wake you, Sheriff,' said Jonas anxiously, fingering the brim of his hat, 'but I'm a mite worried,' Behind him stood Lauri Latimer, her brows knitted in concern, her eyes red-rimmed with grief.

Latimer nodded. 'Aye, lad, it doesn't look too good.' He glanced at his wife. 'Can you get us both a coffee, dear? I reckon we'll be up a while.'

'Yes, Henry. But don't go getting out of bed. You know what the doctor said.'

'Aye, lass, I know.' As his wife stalked downstairs, Latimer said, 'She's taken the shooting hard. Goddammit, the Quincys are our neighbours!' He fixed his gaze on Jonas. 'How's Mrs Quincy doing?'

'Well, as you'd expect, I guess. Friends and townsfolk have rallied round.' He shook his head and glanced away. 'I hated having to tell her. She plumb near fainted in my arms.'

'Poor lass. I aim to get whoever did this, Jonas, even if I am bedridden!'

'You do, Sheriff?'

'Yes! Arrange for all Elliott's friends to come see me tomorrow morning. I want to interview them.'

'What, all at once?'

'No, give them notice, but I want to see them at half-hour intervals.' He pursed his lips. 'This is not good, Jonas. Not good at all! I'm starting to wonder if someone's cooking up something real nasty to spoil my convalescence.'

'You're a damn fine cook,' Virginia said, pushing away her

65

plate with its scattering of cleaned bones. 'Rabbit stew's my favourite!'

'Glad you liked it. Plenty of conies around here.' Daniel opened the glass lantern door and lit two quirlies and passed one to her.

'Thanks.' She flinched as the window to the left of the door crashed noisily and the glass of the oil lamp in front of them was shot to smithereens. Burning oil spread over the table top.

CHAPTER 6

BURNT AROUND THE EDGES

'Get down!' Daniel ordered, grabbing his buckskin coat from the back of his chair. He quickly smothered the flames then ducked under the table with Virginia.

Flickering light from the hearth and the ceiling lantern still illuminated the cabin.

'It might be a couple of hostiles,' Daniel whispered, 'pals of Wolf Slayer—'

'Wolf Slayer?'

'The Sioux I killed.'

'No.' She shook her head. 'It'll be O'Keefe's men – probably Drinkwater.'

The second window shattered and Daniel swore violently. Glancing at her, he added, 'Sorry, but I paid a lot for that glass!'

She touched his arm and forced a fleeting smile.

'Stay put,' he said and crawled to the hearth and grabbed his Henry. It was loaded. He withdrew a box of cartridges and hurried back to her. 'Can you use this?'

'Yes. What are you planning to do?'

'I'll sneak out the back and surprise them.' He grabbed his gunbelt from the chair and pulled out the Army Colt. Feeding a slug into the chamber lined up with the barrel, he said, 'I want you to keep the swine busy.'

'OK.' She nodded. 'I can do that.' She took the rifle and a box of cartridges. Tugging at the dress under her knees, she crawled awkwardly over the floor to the window. Resting her back against the wall, she said, 'Take care, Daniel. I don't want to be a widow afore I'm a wife!' Her heart fluttered at those words then dismissed the memories.

As he slipped behind the cow hide door, she raised herself on one knee and slid the long rifle barrel out the broken window. Attempting to contain her anger, she flinched at a muzzle flash in the darkness then fired.

Daniel moved into the bedroom and opened the door which led out to the privy. He knelt down but could see no feet under the water-closet door. Rushing out, he hid behind the narrow construction. He detected rifle flashes to his right, opposite the front of the shack. He bit back a groan of annoyance as he heard something break, doubtless a porcelain item shot to pieces.

Soundlessly, he moved past the lean-to where he'd stowed the wagon and tethered the horses. In seconds, he was in among the trees and bushes.

Virginia's shots were infrequent, conserving ammo. A little on the high side. Probably worried about hitting me. Damned close shooting, though, he thought, with a measure of proprietary pride.

Moments later, Daniel positioned himself behind the nearest attacker. The gunman wore a grey flat-crowned hat, a leather vest and a red-and-white checked shirt; it wasn't Drinkwater, then. It would be so easy to shoot him

68

in the back. But that wasn't Daniel's way. Besides, he wanted to put a few questions to the varmint.

He crept closer and when he could smell the man's body odour he cocked his Army .44 revolver next to Frank Gordon's ear. The man froze. 'Make any sudden moves and I just might blow a hole in your head,' Daniel warned.

Gordon dropped his rifle. 'Carey! He's got the drop on me!'

At that same instant a shot was fired from the bushes, noisily breaking something else, then silence followed.

'Drinkwater!' Daniel hollered. 'Step out where I can see you!'

No answer.

'The swine!' Gordon groaned. 'I bet he's skedaddled!'

'I don't think I'll take that bet, mister.' Daniel pushed Gordon into the open. 'Virginia!' he called. 'Hold your fire! I'm bringing Gordon with me. And keep a lookout for that snake Drinkwater!'

'Aye, Daniel!' she shouted back.

After tying up Gordon on the hitching rail, Daniel rushed into the trees and searched for a good hour. While there was plenty of sign to show which bushes Drinkwater had hidden behind, there was no trace of him now.

When Daniel returned, Virginia said, 'I don't reckon we're going to sleep tonight. We'll be too busy watching out for Drinkwater.'

Chucking her chin with his enormous hand, Daniel grinned. 'I'd had a mind to stay awake tonight, but for a different reason.'

'You devil!' she whispered.

'Hey,' Gordon interrupted in a rough yet pleading tone, 'what're you two love-birds going to do with me?'

Light slanted over the mountain top and the dawn chorus

of bird-song had started up when Daniel emerged from the cabin. It had been a restless and sleep-deprived night and he felt like kicking Gordon for being the cause. But he couldn't do it. Maybe it had to do with the fact that he woke with a glorious feeling of wellbeing, full in the knowledge that Virginia loved him.

It had been frustrating, sure; as she'd said, 'We've got two years of catch-up to do.' But the lovemaking had to wait. They'd kissed some – which did his heart a power of good – then they agreed to take turns at staying awake.

With the Henry across his knees, he'd watched Virginia sleeping, hair cascading over her face, her long lashes flickering as she dreamed. Despite the tension of the night, and regularly going out to check that Gordon was still tied up, Daniel had savoured the entire dark hours, maybe because he had shared them with Virginia. And when her lookout time came, he'd even caught a fair dusting of sleep.

Gordon was still lashed to the hitching rail.

'Let's go for a chat,' Daniel said, releasing Gordon from the post. The man's hands were still tied behind his back.

'I ain't got anything to say to you, mister.' Gordon spat at the ground.

At least he wasn't foolish enough to spit directly at his captor.

'Let's see, shall we?' Daniel prodded him with the rifle stock and, moving stiffly, Gordon went in front.

For about half an hour they walked into the mountainside forest. Eventually, Daniel said, 'This spot will do.'

Daniel began tying a rope around Gordon's legs.

'What the hell're you doing?'

Ignoring him, Daniel abruptly flung the other end of the rope over a thick tree branch and hauled. Gordon immediately lost his footing and fell jarringly on to his

70

side. 'Hey, what. . . ?'

In a few seconds Gordon was suspended upside down, his head twirling about five feet above the ground.

Daniel started piling sticks and small branches on the ground beneath Gordon's head. It didn't take him long to get a good fire going.

'Hey, you can't do this!'

'I can and I am,' Daniel replied. 'I want you to talk to me.'

Gordon squirmed and jiggled on the end of the rope but he couldn't get away from the choking smoke. 'Go to hell!' He coughed.

'I got this trick from an Indian.'

'So?' Gordon coughed and spat, saliva dribbling on his lip, running up his nose and into his eyes, which started streaming.

Daniel hunkered next to Gordon, stoking the fire with a long stick. 'Cook the enemy's brain in the skull and it tastes real nice. A delicacy. They reckon you take on the victim's intelligence.'

'Don't . . . bother . . . on my account,' Gordon coughed. 'I ain't so bright.'

'Ah, but are you bright enough to tell me what I want to know?'

'You've known Elliott for how long?' Sheriff Latimer asked from his bed.

Edward Pike shifted his feet on the floorboards. 'About four years, Sheriff. Ever since I come here and set up the store.' He nodded, brown eyes weak and watery. 'A good lad and a devoted husband and father, by all accounts. That's my opinion of him as well.'

'Did you go drinking with Elliott much?'

'Only on Friday nights. His wife Annie was understanding like that. Says Elliott needs – needed – man-talk from time to time, what with the house being full o' women an' all.'

'Anyone else with you Friday nights?'

'Slim – Slim Wilson.'

'Yeah, I know Slim – the Wilsons are the Quincys' neighbours.'

'That's right, Sheriff. And Reuben Anson, of course. They've been the best of pals before they even came to Bethesda.'

'Anyone else?'

'Not really. I mean, Elliott was a great guy, he got on with everybody.' Pike paused, thoughtful. 'Your line of questioning, it suggests to me that you're not thinking that Elliott was killed because he was guarding the stage depot, is that right?'

Gesturing with his arms, Latimer said, 'I'm just talking to anybody who knew Elliott. Maybe he had an enemy who would like to see him dead, maybe not.' He shrugged and winced as the wound reminded him why he was bedridden. 'Routine enquiries.'

'Well, I can't think of anybody in that category, Sheriff. As I said, he was liked by most everyone, as far as I knew.'

Latimer smiled. 'Thank you, Eddie, I appreciate you coming on over to talk so early in the day.'

Pike nodded. 'I'm usually around early anyway, on account of my groceries need setting up.'

'Yeah, of course. Still, I appreciate it.'

As the grocer left, Latimer gnashed his teeth and his brow furrowed in thought. Something wasn't right; and that 'something' was burning him up.

'He looks a little burnt around the edges,' Virginia observed when Daniel and Gordon stepped into the clear-

72

ing in front of the cabin.

Arms tied behind his back, Gordon was sullen, his face smoke-blackened and tear-stained.

'You could say I gave him a roasting,' Daniel said. He offered the flicker of a self-satisfied smile. 'Told me everything.'

'He looks a tough customer, Daniel. How'd you manage that?'

Daniel shrugged. 'Told him some nonsense I made up about Indian torture.'

'Why, you lying, no-good, snake-eyed, hame-headed f—'

Virginia pivoted round and slapped Gordon. 'That's enough of that kind of talk, mister.' A hand-impression was left on his cheek. She wiped her sooty palm on Gordon's vest and cocked her head to one side, eyeing Daniel. 'What now?'

'We'll breakfast, then I'll take him back to town. Deputy Johnson can lock him up. Then he can go and arrest O'Keefe.'

She smiled and lifted her skirts, ready to step back on to the veranda. 'I'm going to enjoy seeing that! I'll help with the wagon.'

He reached out and held her arm. 'No, I want you to stay here. There might be a bit of rough house with O'Keefe. I don't want you getting hurt.'

Reluctantly, she agreed to remain behind. She glanced back at the cabin as the cat cried out for food. 'Well, I've got Carson for company.'

'Carson?'

'Kitten – Kit . . . OK?'

Daniel scratched his head. 'There's some logic in it, I suppose.'

'The logic don't add up,' said Henry Latimer, trying and

failing to find a comfortable position in bed.

'What do you mean, Sheriff?' Jonas asked, sitting at the bedside.

'Why would anyone want to shoot Elliott Quincy?'

Jonas shrugged. 'It's got me beat.'

Latimer ignored the comment. 'Elliott was protecting Mrs Monroe from further alleged menacing approaches of Drinkwater and his crowd, isn't that so?'

'Yes. That's the size of it.'

'So killing Elliott don't make sense. It only makes us more vigilant.'

'Yeah, but any death on her doorstep, so to speak, is going to make her uneasy. Maybe she'll sell up now?'

Latimer shook his head. 'Nope. She's made of sterner stuff than that, lad.'

There was a knock on his bedroom door. 'Yeah, who is it?'

'Slim Wilson, Sheriff.' The voice was gruff behind the door. 'I was told to come and speak with you. Mrs Latimer kindly showed me up here.'

Glancing up at Jonas briefly, Latimer said, 'Show him in then leave us.'

'Right, Sheriff.'

Slim entered diffidently, his cap in his hand as if he was being summoned by a particularly irate headmaster. He was overweight with small blue eyes and a cheery disposition that seemed clouded by the moment.

'Come in, Slim – I won't bite!' Latimer barked. 'Sit down and tell me all you know about your late neighbour, Elliott Quincy.'

'Thanks, Sheriff.' He pulled up a chair and it groaned under his bulk. 'We've been drinking buddies since he came to town with his young wife and kid. We still go – most Fridays, if money ain't too tight, that is.'

'Is money tight, Slim?'

Slim nervously tugged at his belt, which clearly was too tight, and shifted in the chair. 'No, business at the sawmill is booming, what with all the new building on the east side of town an' all. Quincy and me both worked for Mr Fitzgerald since he set it up.'

'Good to hear,' said Latimer with a smile.

Slim heaved a great sigh. 'If Mr Fitzgerald hadn't been public spirited, letting Elliott off for community work – deputying – Elliott would be alive today. It don't seem right, do it?'

'No, son, it don't. The blame rests with the cowardly gunman, nobody else. It weren't the Lord's work, either—'

'The Devil's, more like.'

'Maybe so, maybe so . . . I have to ask, Slim – where were you on that fateful night?'

'Me?' Latimer nodded. 'I was helping Mr Fitzgerald in the mill – on account of work falling behind since Elliott was deputying.'

'Thank you, Slim. Send in Reuben, if he's waiting, will you?'

Standing up quickly, Slim knocked over the chair. 'Yes, Sheriff.' He righted the chair and left, seeming pleased to get this little ordeal over with.

This was getting to be a knotty problem, Latimer thought.

Daniel tied Gordon belly down over the back of a buggy horse and fastened its reins to his cantle. As he mounted his own horse, Virginia came up to him.

She gripped the bridle. 'Now don't do anything rash.'

'That sounds real fine. It's a long time since anyone cared for me one way or another.'

Even upside down, Gordon managed to grimace. 'Oh, please!'

Virginia slapped his cheek and he yelped. 'It's rude to eavesdrop!'

Turning back to Daniel, she leaned up and he bent down, leather creaking. They kissed briefly.

'I'll be waiting,' she said.

All the way to town Daniel kept a wary eye out for Drinkwater, waiting to be ambushed. He breathed a sigh of relief as the trail came out on Front Street. He rode past the schoolhouse on the corner and the church opposite on the other side of Main Street.

Mrs McCall was pruning her cherry tree and paused to stare briefly at him and his captive; then she waved.

Jonas Johnson was sitting on the veranda in front of the sheriff's office. His jaw dropped when he saw Gordon slung over the trailing horse.

Running over, Johnson said, 'What's up with Frank?'

'Gordon and Drinkwater tried to shoot us in my cabin. Virginia and me.'

Johnson took off his hat and scratched his brow. 'Where's Drinkwater? He ain't dead, is he?'

'No, but what's it to you if he is?'

'Well, a death has to be accounted for, you know. It's the law.'

Turning in his saddle, Daniel said, 'Is the law going to lock up this man for shooting out my windows and damn-near killing me and Miss Virginia?'

Putting his hat on, Johnson said, 'Well, let's get the guy off of that critter first.'

Two blocks down, the swing doors of The Gem opened and Royce O'Keefe strode out. He passed the cobbler's shop and climbed up the steps of the boardwalk in front of the sheriff's office. 'What the hell's happened to Frank, Deputy?'

While he loosened the ropes securing Gordon, Johnson thumbed at Daniel. 'He's accusing Frank of shooting up his place.'

Glaring directly at Daniel, O'Keefe snarled, 'And are there any witnesses?'

'Yep,' said Daniel. 'Miss Virginia Simone, for one. Me for another. And my broke windows for a third.'

Staring up and down the street, O'Keefe said, 'I don't see Miss Simone anywhere. Seems to me it's just your word agin Frank's!'

Gently rubbing his chafed wrists, Frank Gordon said, 'He's lyin', Deputy. I reckon he's drunk too much liquor and imagining things.'

Turning to the deputy, O'Keefe demanded, 'Let my man go, Jonas, or you won't hear the last of this!'

Thin-lipped, Johnson nodded. 'You can go, Frank. But not far, you hear? I reckon the sheriff might want to talk to you later.'

'Thanks, Jonas!' He walked to The Gem alongside O'Keefe, laughing as they went.

'It looks like I made a wasted journey,' Daniel said.

'I'm sorry, but O'Keefe's right. And he's in a foul mood today.'

'His mood has nothing to do with me,' Daniel observed innocently.

'You gave one of his men a sound beating, looks like to me. He don't take kindly to that kind of thing.'

'Gordon had it coming to him. I've got to replace windows and all.'

Johnson shrugged. 'Your word agin his. You should've brought Virginia in with you. As a witness, she'd be enough for me to hold Gordon. As it is. . . .' He shrugged.

At that moment Ruth Monroe crossed the road from the general store. 'Deputy Johnson, my brother's gone missing.'

Jonas flushed and couldn't seem to hold her eyes with his. Peering towards the southern end of the street, he suggested, 'Have you tried the cat-house?'

'How dare you suggest—' She paused and blushed. 'I suppose my altercation with that woman is all round town by now?'

Taking off his hat, Jonas said, 'Yes, ma'am. Sorry. I don't suppose you'd want to visit the Bella Union?'

'Of course not!'

'No – I'm sorry, Ruth – Mrs Monroe. . . .'

'I'll go, ma'am,' volunteered Daniel.

'Thank you.'

'I'll check Ma Simpson's,' Johnson added and all three strode down the main street as the sun climbed to promise another hot day.

'Fine day for a funeral, Reuben,' Latimer said, as the young man entered the bedroom.

'Not if it's your best pal, Sheriff.' Reuben Anson looked sullen and clearly hadn't slept well; the puffiness under his steel-grey eyes testified to that.

'How long have you known Elliott?'

Reuben's face twisted in thought as he nonchalantly pulled up the chair and reversed it, sitting with his arms on the back. 'Eight, no, nine years, I reckon.'

'Did you both come to Bethesda Falls together?'

'No, I came about two years after Elliott and Annie had settled here. Four years or so back. Why?'

'Just wondered.'

'Wondered what, Sheriff?'

'How come you wound up here, of all places? I mean,

Elliott's doing nicely at the mill, the pair of them have a lovely daughter. What was the attraction?'

'Attraction?' Reuben smiled, the lips thin. 'I don't know what you mean. It was by chance. I was passing through, I saw Annie Quincy in the general store and we got to chatting and I called on Elliott.' He leaned back. 'As old pals do, you know?'

'Yeah, life's full of coincidences, Reuben. Say, where were you at the time of the shooting?'

Reuben ran a hand through his cornhusk hair. 'Stopping over at Elliott's, as a matter of fact. Annie'd planned a late supper when he came off deputy duty. I was asked to tag along.'

'Who'll verify that?'

'Well, Mrs Quincy, I guess. I was in the kitchen when Jonas brought the bad news.'

'Jonas never mentioned that fact.'

'Must have slipped his mind, Sheriff. You know what he's like. Anything else? I only ask, as I told Mrs Quincy I'd pick up the groceries for her.' He smiled. 'She's preparing food for the mourners.'

'Aye, she's a plucky lass,' Latimer said. 'No, that's all for now, Reuben. Thanks.'

Reuben stood and swivelled the chair round. 'I'm sorry I wasn't much help, Sheriff. But as anyone will tell you, Elliott didn't have an enemy in the world. And I should know, being his best pal.'

It seemed that Daniel had acquired several best pals as he walked into the ornate foyer of the Bella Union. He immediately attracted three calico queens. Dresses swishing silkily, they glided towards him, a strong sickly-sweet aroma hovering around them.

Though feeling slightly uncomfortable to be the centre

of so much attention, he fired several questions at them. He got plenty of answers, but not the kind he wanted to hear. Nobody had seen Saul Barchus since yesterday.

He ran a finger round his bandanna, glad to leave.

Outside, he met Johnson and Ruth Monroe. Their long faces conveyed bad news.

The deputy said, 'No sign of him at Ma Simpson's, either.'

'Thanks, Deputy,' Ruth said. She shook his hand – a dismissal.

'Ma'am,' he replied, and doffed his hat then turned away with some reluctance.

As Jonas walked off to Main Street, she glanced up at Daniel. 'Will you escort me home, Mr McAlister?'

'Yes, ma'am.'

When they got to the depot, Ruth went in first and offered him a coffee.

'That would be appreciated, ma'am,' he said as she moved ahead of him, along the passage and into the kitchen. 'Then I've got to get back—'

Ruth screamed.

He reached the kitchen door. She was standing next to the table, shaking from head to toe.

'What's the matter, Mrs Monroe?'

She thrust a sheet of paper at him. 'This . . . this. . . .'

He took it and read, 'Sell up. Get out of town. If you want to see your brother alive again.'

'Someone has been *in here* and left *that* note,' she said, stating the obvious. He'd been able to work out that much himself.

She sank on to a ladder-backed chair and put her head in her arms and sobbed.

Daniel felt awkward. He wanted to offer comfort, but it wasn't his place to do that. Besides, he should be getting back to Virginia.

'I'd be happy to stay and find out where Saul's gone, ma'am, only—'

'You would?' She lifted her gaze, eyes and cheeks glistening. 'I'd be thankful for that, sir.'

'Only I have to get back to my cabin first. I've left Virginia all alone out there and it's her first night. I don't feel comfortable doing that.'

Uncomfortably slung belly-down over a mule, Saul Barchus groaned at each juddering movement as they climbed the old mountain track. On either side of him was a mounted man, each of them as big as him. His head ached and he couldn't remember much after slipping out the back of the depot to speak with Erica about her being pregnant.

He wouldn't care so much if the head was sore because he'd had a good time with plenty of liquor. But it was so long ago that he couldn't recall the last evening he'd over-indulged. He'd learned soon enough that Ruth didn't abide that kind of behaviour. At least being sober of a night he got to wake up most mornings feeling fresh and ready for the day's toil. And he had to give his sister credit, she worked as hard as any two men. It was a sad time when she lost Dillon; she mourned her husband for a day then seemed to lose herself in work, plugging away twice as hard, as if to make up for her man's absence.

It wasn't difficult for Saul to determine that they were moving along one of several goat-trails up Grimm Mountain. But what were these men doing?

Saul was consoled with the thought that if they'd wanted to kill him, they could have done so long before now and tipped his body down any one of countless anonymous gullies. Why they'd made him their prisoner was a complete mystery.

He'd just have to bide his time. And suffer the uncomfortable ride.

Maybe the answers to his questions would arise when they got to their destination.

For a brief moment Saul thought he detected a slight movement in the trees. As if a pair of eyes – grey-green? – studied him and his captors. A timber wolf, maybe.

CHAPTER 7

"WHAT A WASTE!"

A wolf howled in the mountains and Virginia shuddered then chided herself over the reaction. It wasn't as if she hadn't heard them before. But living out here, alone, they seemed closer, more threatening. She was a town-girl, not a backwoods woman. Maybe she was having second thoughts. She looked down at her hands. They were fine, manicured, with long tapering fingers. A card-sharp's hands. They hadn't always been so good-looking, she recalled. She'd been married for three years, after all. Toiling over kitchen pots and pans, washing laundry in every kind of weather. Then, her hands had been mostly red, but sometimes chapped or blue. And the nails had been cracked or jagged-edged, not like the virtual talons she possessed now.

Ten years ago this fall, she realized with a shock. She and a number of others in their wagon train had survived the raid. But the marauding Indians had killed many settlers, including her husband Bud, and their two-year-old son, Steven.

One of the remaining families – the Mayos, kindly God-fearing folk – took her in, helped her mourn. She retained her married name but referred to herself as 'Miss'. At their destination she parted company with the Mayos and met up with a gambler and card-sharp, Gideon Pointer. He taught her all he knew as they worked on the steamboat plying the Missouri between St Louis and St Joseph – a journey that encompassed six days there and six back, full of boredom that was relieved by gambling and liquor. They split five years back, in San Francisco and she met O'Keefe, who had dreams of building a gambling empire. For some odd reason, he wanted to start at Bethesda Falls. Less competition, that's for sure. She had enough money and savvy to insist on a purely business relationship and it suited him, since she was the best wheel-of-fortune woman in the territory.

Now she looked around the cabin, determined not to compare the place with the richly appointed saloons she had frequented. In fact the cabin was homely enough, she supposed. The layer of dust was only a few days old. But she'd have to talk Daniel into buying material for curtains. And those windows. He seemed really upset about them being shot to hell. Probably waited weeks for the glass to be delivered to the trading post he'd mentioned.

She'd spent the day sweeping up the fragments, cleaning the table top and picking flowers to decorate the rooms. Bread and cheese mustered for lunch. Carson was happy with a left-over meat-covered bone, though he found it difficult to manipulate with only one front paw. As she watched the cat her stomach rumbled and she reckoned dusk wasn't far off.

Where was Daniel?

She prayed he was all right. O'Keefe wasn't a back-shooter, but he was a tough *hombre* and liked to get his own way.

Virginia paced up and down and then went outside and

stood on the veranda, smoking a cigarette, gazing at the trail entrance in the trees. Birds flew by. Some sang. A whippoorwill called. She felt lonely now. Stepping inside, she shut and bolted the door.

Light the ceiling lantern. Warm the place up – as if she needed to in July, for landsakes. She laughed. It was hot, oppressively so, yet she shivered. With fear.

She lit the lantern and its mellow glow made her feel a little better. About half an hour passed then Carson cried to be let out. She stood up, went to the door, unbolted and opened it. Carson limped outside, away from the spillage of light, to do his business. She leaned against the doorpost and peered at the sky. The moon was full; it was a glorious night, to be shared with your lover: where was Daniel? But she couldn't fret for long, she was entranced by so many stars.

The shot rang out and, as she tumbled back through the doorway into the cabin, she saw stars; then everything went as black as the space in between them.

A minute later, Drinkwater stepped on to the veranda and leaned against the open door. He levelled his rifle at Virginia's still form on the floor, but she didn't move. There was a splatter of blood by her shoulder. 'What a waste,' he said, shaking his head and stepping over her.

He lifted the lid of the chest on the right and pulled out clothes and a few books, discarding them on the floor. He opened the trunk next to it and shut it immediately, recognizing Virginia's clothes. He ransacked the dresser's drawers, tipping out all their contents. Grim-faced, he tore down the cow hide and strode into the bedroom. His eyes widened at sight of the padlocked chest at the foot of the bed. He stepped back a safe distance and shot the lock away.

Drinkwater lifted the lid. 'That's more like it!' Grabbing

a gunny sack, he untied the thin rope. Inside was Daniel McAlister's winnings. He rummaged amid more clothes and boxes and found two small sacks of gold. Sure, O'Keefe would get his money back; but he wouldn't get the gold, Drinkwater reckoned, shoving the sacks into his pockets. Nope. He straightened up and moved back into the living room. Perks, for services rendered, he thought, and again eyed Virginia. That's one perk he'd have liked. . . .

Still, no point in leaving any evidence. He picked up the lantern by its handle and opened the oil reservoir. He spilled oil over the floor, splashing Virginia's dress. Finally, he threw down the lamp by the front door, where the glass shattered and kerosene burst into flame.

The fire quickly spread.

'Sheer waste,' he said and slammed the door shut.

Draughts of air through the broken windows wafted the flames and fed them.

The musky sage-scent of dusk wafted down Main Street as Daniel mounted his horse outside the stage depot. Impatient to get away, he eased the chestnut round, facing north to head out of town. Ruth watched anxiously from the doorway.

'Daniel! Daniel McAlister!'

He recognized the voice of Deputy Jonas Johnson and glanced over his shoulder. The deputy was running along the boardwalk, waving an arm, holding aloft a sheet of paper.

Reining in, Daniel steadied his horse and dismounted, waiting for the deputy.

'What's the problem, Jonas?' he asked, friendly enough. He gestured at the paper Jonas was holding. 'You got some news for me?'

'Yeah,' said Jonas, rather sheepishly, 'and it's bad.'

'Oh, what is it?'

'It's a warrant for your arrest.'

'My arrest?' Daniel took a step back and raised a hand to stroke the snout of his horse which bridled at his tone of astonishment. 'You're joshing me, aren't you?'

Jonas shook his head. 'I wish I was, Daniel. But the mayor's authorized it till the judge gets here. A witness saw you do it. I'm sorry.'

'Do it? Do what, for God's sake?' he said in an exasperated tone.

'Eh? Oh, I'm arresting you for the murder of Elliott Quincy.'

Behind them, Ruth gasped.

Daniel laughed aloud. 'You think I shot that poor lad in the back?'

'It ain't what I think, Daniel.' His eyes implored Daniel to understand his predicament. 'It's what my witness says.'

'Who's this witness?' Daniel asked coldly.

'Frank Gordon.'

Again Daniel laughed. 'You're going to believe *him*, after all? Earlier today, you let him go—'

'Well, he and Greg Bartlett have sworn to witnessing you do the shooting.'

Daniel nodded. 'I see Gordon's learnt his lesson. It ain't just my word against his now, is it?'

Jonas shook his head. 'No, it ain't. Bartlett corroborates the testimony.'

'He would, wouldn't he?' Daniel was tempted to punch Jonas in the face and mount his horse and ride away. By now Virginia would be anxious about his whereabouts. But he couldn't do it. No matter how contrived the accusation appeared to him, he couldn't flout the law, even if it was in the relatively ineffectual guise of Jonas Johnson. Daniel sighed and nodded. 'You'd better arrest me, then, hadn't you?'

'Yes . . . yes, I was about to do that.' He stepped forward and his eyes couldn't hold Daniel's. 'I'm sorry.'

Daniel nodded and handed over his Colt. 'What about my horse?'

Jonas shoved the weapon in his belt. 'I'll take it to the livery, once I've got you in the hoosegow.'

'Thanks. I appreciate that.'

'Why'd you have to be so nice about it all?' Jonas remonstrated. 'I feel bad about this as it is!'

'OK, Deputy, just read me the riot act, or whatever it is you have to do to make it legal.'

Marcy sat in The Gem reading his newspaper, apparently minding his own business. From his vantage point at the rear of the saloon, he was able to see everyone in the room. He had recognized Greg Bartlett as soon as the man entered. Bartlett was accompanied by a man with a florid complexion and hair that looked slightly singed. The pair of them had propped up the bar for a good hour and were well into their cups when their conversation took an interesting turn. Marcy listened attentively.

'Let's have another one, Frank,' said Bartlett, chuckling. 'We deserve it after today!'

'Aye, I don't like helping out the law, but this time it serves the swine right!' Frank Gordon shivered, as if someone had walked over his grave, and brushed a hand through black hair that was oddly stringy like twine. 'McAlister should be hanged for what he did to me!'

'Well, he's behind bars now, so let's celebrate, eh?'

The name pricked Marcy's ears. That was the man who'd very likely saved the lives of all the passengers on the stage – including his.

Careful to stay concealed behind the newspaper, Marcy listened and, the more he heard, the more his lips curved in a knowing smile.

Sheriff Henry Latimer wasn't smiling. His face looked like thunder. 'You've arrested Daniel McAlister because of what Frank Gordon says?'

'I had no choice, Sheriff. He had corroboration from Bartlett—'

'Corroboration? You can't even spell it!' Latimer's face was suffused purple.

'Now, Henry, calm down,' his wife advised. 'No point in getting all riled up. It's late.'

Letting out a gushing sigh, Latimer lay back in the bed and his chest sent a stabbing painful reminder about his condition. 'You're right as usual, dear,' he said, and held Lauri's hand.

Surprised at his even tone, he asked Jonas, 'Shouldn't you have questioned both of them, to see if their stories tallied?'

'I thought about it, Sheriff, but I haven't done much in the way of interrogation of witnesses, you know.'

'It isn't interrogation,' said Latimer, 'just questioning.'

'Unless it's the sheriff doing the questioning,' Lauri chimed in.

He gave her a severe look. 'Why *were* they there, anyway?'

'I didn't get round to asking them that yet, Sheriff.'

Before he could explode again, Latimer was distracted by the doorbell ringing. He detected relief on his deputy's face.

'I'll go and see who might be calling at this time of night,' his wife said and moved to the door, where she stopped. 'Now don't go getting annoyed while I'm gone, Henry Latimer!' she warned and stepped out of the bedroom.

Latimer glowered at his deputy. 'You've got to start think-ing on your feet, Jonas. I won't always be here.' He coughed. 'Hell, I almost wasn't. If that slug had been a shade to the right, I'd now be dead as a can of corned beef!'

Jonas shook his head and glanced down at the floor. 'Honest to God, Sheriff, I don't know if I'm cut out to be a lawman.' He held up a hand, as if he was about to take an oath. 'I want to do my bit for the community, but I ain't sure now if—'

'We all have doubts, lad, from time to time. Face them down.' Latimer wafted a hand to and fro. 'You've got the sand, I'm sure of it. Your heart's in the right place too.'

'It's my heart I'm worried about. I hate the thought that Elliott was working for me when he was gunned down. I have these feelings for Mrs Monroe but I don't rightly know if I can face her now, after what's happened. . . .'

Latimer arched an eyebrow at this revelation. He strug-gled to sit up and leaned forward. 'Have you questioned her about the shooting?'

'What?' Jonas said, looking up. 'No, of course not, Sheriff. She was indoors at the time.'

Biting his lip on a caustic remark, Latimer cursed his wife for her common sense and sank back against the pillows.

The door opened and his wife said, 'Henry, there's a Mr Marcy to see you.' She stepped to one side, her hands primly clasped to the front.

Marcy entered. 'Good evening, gents. I was told you were both here,' he said, eyeing them, 'and I thought that since I've acquired some knowledge pertinent to the arrest of Mr Daniel McAlister, it was my public-spirited duty to inform you at the first opportunity.'

'Spit it out, damn it!' Latimer said.

'Henry! That's no way to talk to a guest in our home.'

*

Although there had been no formal introductions, Saul had learned that his two abductors were called Roy and Wes. No surnames. As night fell they sat at a small square table, drinking forty-rod and playing seven up with greasy pasteboard cards. Their stake was a small pile of greenbacks between them.

They didn't seem to pay Saul any attention, which wasn't surprising, since he wasn't going anywhere. His hands were tightly tied behind his back and his shoulders and upper arms were stiff due to the constraints and inactivity. His face throbbed where the stitches in his cheek were coming loose; he could feel a faint trickle of blood dribbling down his chin. He sat on the dusty floor of the abandoned cabin, resting his back against the wall.

The place was probably built and used by fur trappers, when, a long time ago, there was money to be had in that business. The market had been saturated or the critters hunted to near-extinction; one way or another, fur trapping was now just a sideline activity.

It had taken him a long time to prise out a nail from the wooden plank board and now he was attempting to use it to cut through the rope. His fingers and wrists ached and he had to stop from time to time for a rest, though he despaired at every second that he wasted; individual strands of the rope were frayed, at least.

'I've been wondering, Wes, why d'you think Smith wants us to bring this Barchus fella here?'

Wes flipped up the last of his seven cards and it completed his run of ace through seven. He grinned, displaying crooked teeth. 'Less wondering and more concentration on the cards, Roy, and you might win the odd hand!'

'Well, you was always better than me at cards. I got the luck with the ladies, though!'

91

'You call them ladies?' Wes let out a guffaw.

Roy scowled. 'You ain't answered my question.'

'Well, it stands to reason. He don't want Barchus found in town by no search-party.'

'Yeah, but why kidnap him in the first place?'

Wes smiled. 'Zachary Smith wants the stage depot. The note I left told his sister straight – get out, or she won't see her brother alive again.'

Dealing a fresh hand of seven cards, Roy nodded. 'I wondered what that note said. So when she leaves town, our job's done?'

'Our job's done already. We've been paid. You've already lost half of it playing your lousy losing hands!'

'So what do we do with Barchus?'

'Out here, a body could stay lost forever.'

'Lost? We ain't lost.'

'No, but I've been thinking as well.' Wes leaned across the table and jerked a thumb in Saul's direction. 'That man can identify us to the law. If we let him live, we can't go back to Bethesda Falls.'

Roy gave a startled gasp. 'Hey, I hadn't thought about that!'

'Right. So we've gotta consider – do we want to go back to that town?'

'I see what you mean. Since we've been paid, we can hightail it someplace else and leave this fella here till he escapes or rots. Or we can get rid of him permanent like and return to town where nobody'd be any the wiser.'

'That's the way I see it, Roy. Life's full of difficult choices, ain't it?'

Saul's blood ran cold.

CHAPTER 8

SLEIGHT-OF-HAND

By the time that Marcy had repeated verbatim what Frank
Gordon and Greg Bartlett had said in the saloon, Sheriff
Latimer was all set to swing his legs out of bed and strap
on his gunbelt, and the trifling matter of getting dressed
could go hang! Instead, by a stupendous effort of
willpower he desisted from giving in to this urge and
groaned loudly.

Jonas said, 'I'll go and release McAlister at once,
Sheriff.'

A glance was exchanged between Latimer and his wife.
'Yes, do that. But tell the man that I want to see him. And
he can stay here in the spare room tonight. It's far too late
to go riding off into the mountains now.'

'Right, Sheriff.'

When his deputy had left, Latimer addressed Marcy:
'You don't think they were just too drunk and boasting
about some imaginary stuff?'

'No, Sheriff, I've studied their kind before.' Marcy
adjusted his eye-glasses. 'They revel in their unlawfulness.
If they can put one over the lawmakers, they'll do it. From
what I could gather, the impetus probably was spite on

93

behalf of the one called Frank Gordon. He doesn't seem to take kindly to Daniel McAlister.'

'No, and from what Jonas tells me, I'm not surprised at that either!'

'This is a pleasant surprise, Sheriff,' Daniel said, as he entered the bedroom, his gunbelt now restored to his waist.

'You owe your release to Mr Marcy here,' Latimer said, gesturing.

Marcy stepped forward and they shook hands. 'One good turn deserves another,' Marcy said.

'I thank you both,' Daniel said, 'but I need to be getting back to my cabin. Miss Simone will be having kittens over my absence.'

'How is that poor cat, by the way?' Latimer asked, his eyes twinkling.

'Coping. If he was a horse, I'd've shot him. I guess he has a few of his nine lives left.'

'Well, the cat'll keep Miss Simone company, won't it?'

'Well, I guess so,' Daniel said, though he felt sure that she'd welcome his company more – for some of that promised 'catch-up', he hoped – but he couldn't very well say that.

'It's late, Daniel. My wife's only too happy to put you up for the night. You can get on the trail at first light.'

At that moment Mrs Latimer entered. 'I heard mention of my name.' She smiled at Marcy and Daniel. 'I've got some pecan pie I'm trying to get rid of, too.'

Daniel smiled and licked his lips. 'Well, that's mighty decent of you, Sheriff, ma'am.'

'And you're welcome to a bite to eat, Mr Marcy.'

'Don't mind if I do, ma'am.' Marcy beamed.

Daniel stayed the night and was up, dressed and on the

trail at sun-up, together with the spare horse.

Leaning close to Wes, Roy said, conspiratorially, 'There's something else, I reckon.'

'Oh, really? What's that?'

'If we keep Barchus alive, maybe we could get a ransom out of Widow Monroe.'

Wes slapped his thigh. 'Well, damn me, if that ain't a splendid idea!'

'Lure her up here with the money ... and, you know. . . .' Roy gestured crudely.

Wes chuckled. 'That's a bonus, ain't it? Maybe we could demand five thousand bucks, eh?'

'No, wait, that's an odd number, it don't divide into two.'

'Of course it does, that's two and a half grand each.'

'Oh, right.'

'That'll keep us for the rest of our miserable lives!'

'Yep, that's a tidy sum.' Roy laughed. 'I don't usually get ideas. I'm quite proud of that one.'

Saul had been tempted to tell them to go to hell. Besides, Ruth didn't have that kind of money. But he thought better of it. No point in tempting fate. He kept quiet after that and concentrated on trying to escape, fretting at the rope with the rusted nail.

The flames had died down by the time Daniel returned to his cabin or what was left of it, which wasn't much. The water closet was scorched and had half-collapsed; the stone fireplace supported a couple of blackened rafters and that was all there was in an upright position. The flames had even reached the lean-to and ruined the buckboard. At least the remaining horse had broken loose and was grazing at the edge of the copse of trees.

While he let the cinders cool off, he scoured the ground encircling the place, his heart heavy. At the trail entrance at the far end of the clearing, he knelt down and identified a couple of fresh scuff-marks – from a shod horse. Must be Drinkwater, he mused, gritting his teeth.

Finally, he found a suitably long branch and used it to jab at the burnt detritus. The bedroom chest was scorched and partially intact – but everything inside was either burnt to a crisp or missing; he couldn't tell which was the case. There was very little left of Virginia's trunk. He wondered what she'd lost – probably all her worldly goods. Just like him, he supposed, though he didn't set much store on possessions.

His heart lightened a little. There was no sign of any corpse.

If Virginia hadn't perished in the fire, then what had happened to her – and the cat?

The cat licking her face had brought Virginia back to consciousness. She felt pain in the back of her head and in her shoulder and coughed, finding it difficult to breathe. Startled by the smoke, she sat up and cried out as she felt the intense heat on her legs. Flames were licking at the hem of her skirt! With the flat of her hand, she frantically beat at the blaze. Wincing at the frightful pain, she eventually smothered the fire on her dress.

Smoke filled the cabin. Burning floorboards prevented her reaching the windows, front door or the bedroom. Through the swathing smoke and licking flames she spotted her trunk, already burning brightly. She couldn't get anywhere near it, the heat was too intense. The two precious daguerreotypes of her with Bud and baby Steven, taken before they set out with the wagon train, were burning – lost! She let out a piercing scream of frustration and anger and absently raised a hand to her throbbing fore-head; it came away with blood. What had happened? She didn't know. She remembered standing on the veranda, waiting for Daniel – then nothing.

Coughing on the smoke, she hugged the kitten to her chest. Trapped. She was trapped!

Trap-door – that was it!

Moving unsteadily, her head still pounding from the bullet-graze, she held tightly on to the cat and crawled across the floor. Flinging away the animal rug, she left the cat wrapped in her shawl and stood up.

The trap-door was heavy and she felt quite giddy and weak. She persevered though and, straining her back muscles, she heaved it up.

A welcoming draught of cool air rushed up to meet her. Holding the cat in her shawl, she climbed down. She could only glimpse the odd stone or the sparkle of water as flames reflected. Her boot slipped on a wet rock and she fell and her backside slithered over bruising stones, her free hand futilely attempting to stop her down-rushing movement. The slippery rocks, the powerful stream and the darkness disoriented her.

Virginia was shoved left and right, until she banged her head and lost consciousness.

Daniel knelt amid the ashes, his big hands black as coal as he lifted something that once resembled a book. He threw it down and a small puff of black ash erupted. Everything lost! All he'd worked for, all he had, save for the clothes on his back.

He assumed that Virginia had been abducted by Drinkwater, but there was no evidence. The scant horse tracks were on rock; if only they'd been on soft earth, he could have distinguished the arrival tracks against those departing; if the leaving impressions were deeper, then the rider was carrying a much heavier load.

It was so frustrating! He kicked at the undergrowth and paused, his eye having caught something.

Kneeling down, he checked – the soil here, it was softer. Two boot-prints, approaching the clearing. The heel was well defined. And the prints were fresh. They ain't mine, he thought, so whose are they? He glared at the dense forest foliage, his jaw tight.

None of this devastation amounted to a hill of beans, so long as Virginia was all right. His stomach clenched. What the hell had happened to her? Where was she?

Virginia recovered consciousness in a strange-smelling enclosed space, the air filled with wood-smoke. Her head pounded insistently. She sat up with a start, panicking for a second, fearing she was still in the burning cabin. But she could see a small circle of starlit sky above, beyond a cluster of wooden poles.

A firm yet gentle hand restrained – yet startled – her.

'Be calm, you are safe,' said the man, his voice deep and gentle with a slight foreign inflection. Light was poor, but she saw several feathers sticking out from the man's head. Black braided hair, adorned with coloured beads, hung down past his cheeks. His clothing – buckskin jacket and leggings – appeared white and there was a slight aura that seemed to surround him.

'You're an Indian – but you speak my language?'

He chuckled. 'We Indians as you call us are not savages. We're quite capable of learning your tongue, though sadly most of your people cannot be troubled to learn ours.'

She knew that she was in a tent of some kind; the walls seemed to be made from hide. It was stifling inside, but strangely comforting too. 'Where am I?'

'My lodge is a place of safety in the mountain forest.'

'Grimm Mountain?'

'It goes by that name, I believe.'

She experienced a vivid flash of memory and her hand darted to her head. There was a damp poultice on her wound.

Then, his big hands, which had been visible all the time, swirled slightly and, as if out of nowhere, he produced Carson, her cat. 'He has been fed. He's a lucky little animal.'

Impressed by the Indian's sleight-of-hand, she hugged the cat to her. 'Thank you – what's your name?'

'In your tongue it is White Buffalo Calf. What is yours?'

She told him then lowered the cat to the blanket-covered floor.

'I'll leave you to get reacquainted with your pet.' White Buffalo Calf moved the tent flap aside.

She glanced up. 'No, don't go. I'd appreciate your company.' She fished inside her skirt and pulled out the pea and shells. 'Tell me about yourself, if you wish, while I amuse Carson here.'

'Carson?' White Buffalo Calf chuckled. 'Kit Carson?'

She nodded.

'Most amusing!'

As they talked, Carson would watch her put a pea under a shell, yet when he pawed at the shell, the pea was gone!

White Buffalo Calf laughed. 'Your hands are as deft as mine.'

Before long, they were exchanging notes on magic tricks and concealment. While they did this, Virginia told him about Daniel, the attack and the fire.

Sagely, White Buffalo Calf said, 'We are fortunate that the fire did not spread to the forest. Your man built sensibly.'

All night Saul had worked at the rope and when daylight streamed through the single window, he couldn't believe he'd managed to stay awake so long. Finally, when he sensed the tension give, he felt almost light-headed. The section of rope he'd cut apart meant he could free his wrists. The pain was excruciating as circulation started to flow. His backside, shoulders and arms were aching. And his head still throbbed.

Roy sat at the table, playing solitaire or something with the cards. Wes lay snoring on the bunk at the rear of the shack.

Saul had to make a move soon, before he had two of them to contend with. Two rifles rested against the wall by the bunk; a gunbelt hung from the bed-head post. And Roy's revolver was on the table, by his right hand.

He'd have to get up, spring towards Roy, incapacitate him and get out before Wes woke and collected his wits. Or he could try knocking out Roy and falling on Wes before the man knew what was happening.

For a man of his size, it shouldn't have been difficult. Unfortunately, Saul had always been big – and docile. His presence invariably meant nobody tried anything with him, so he was never in any fights. He had lots of friends at school too. In adulthood, things had panned out differently, since a man wasn't necessarily measured by his build but by his willingness to shoot down any opponent. Saul hated guns.

If he could get out of the shack, he stood a chance. Inside, it was two armed men against him and he knew that he'd lose.

Roy yawned and leaned back on his chair, tipping it on its rear legs; he stretched his arms out to unkink some muscles. Saul would have liked to do the same but there was no time. Slowly, silently, he brought his hands round from behind his back, pressed down on the floor to give himself purchase and pushed himself up, the stiffness in his legs surprisingly chronic.

Out of the corner of his eye Roy saw the movement and swivelled round. His eyes started and his mouth gaped open. Vital seconds. Ignoring the pain and aches, Saul launched himself at Roy, almost flying across the floor-space, and bashed full into Roy at the same instant as the man grabbed his revolver.

The pair of them crashed into the table and it collapsed under their weight, along with Roy's chair. A splinter of wood lanced up and pierced Roy's left forearm and he yelled in agony.

Without conscious volition, Saul regained his feet and manhandled the table top. He swung it round, thrusting its edge forcefully into the throat of the awakening Wes.

Then he swirled round and lurched to the door, pulling it open. He stumbled out into fresh air, staggered two paces and almost fell to his death.

The damned shack was on the very lip of a chasm. Why would any fool build a place here? He peered down. The shack hadn't originally been this close to the edge. The ground had fallen away – a long-ago rock slide, probably. Scree and a jumble of boulders sloped beneath him. He heard shouting behind – they wouldn't be too considerate since he'd hurt them. He shouldn't have run, he should have fought, while he'd had the advantage. But his limbs had barely responded. The pair of them would soon have overpowered him in the confines of the shack.

Even as he moved, his legs were stiff and hurt at every step, but he walked unsteadily to the right, towards a cluster of rocks and foliage.

Hide, must hide!

Saul plunged into the trees and two bullets zipped over-head, dislodging branches and leaves.

Daniel hunkered down by the stream and lifted two hand-fuls of red mud from the bank. Returning to the track, he poured the sludge into one of the foot-prints. Carefully, he patted the mud, flattening it.

On top of the mud he placed dry wood and grass then finally set it alight.

A bullfrog nearby made a chug-a-rum sound. There was something else, though – he detected it above the crack-ling flames and wood, above the noise of forest and stream. He stood and, drawing his Colt, swung round.

An Indian entered the clearing and in one arm he carried Carson the cat; beside him stood Virginia.

Daniel's heart leapt as she ran to him.

'Oh, Daniel,' she sobbed, 'your lovely cabin – all gone!'

He enfolded her in his arms.

After a moment, she let go and stared at the little fire he'd just made. 'What are you doing? I'd have thought this place has seen enough fire.'

He nodded. 'I'll tell you in a minute.' He nodded at the Indian who hadn't moved from the edge of the clearing; the man stood in his white buckskins, erect and dignified. 'Who's your friend?'

Virginia explained then added, 'White Buffalo Calf's a medicine man. He's from the same tribe as Wolf Slayer.' She screwed up her eyes. 'For some reason he won't speak Wolf Slayer's name. Goes all round the houses to avoid it, seems to me. Anyway, after a while I gathered who he was talking about.'

'It's considered bad luck to speak the name of the dead.'

'Oh. Really?'

'Yes.' He took her hand and walked up to White Buffalo Calf. 'I come in peace,' he said in Lakota, holding up a hand, palm outward. 'I wish to thank you for saving my woman.'

The medicine man held up his hand and nodded. 'Your woman is brave. I say this in my tongue to avoid embarrassing her.'

'Thank you, though I'm sure she would be pleased to hear you say that about her.' He looked directly into the medicine man's dark glinting eyes. 'I'm sorry I killed the warrior.'

White Buffalo Calf nodded. 'I saw.'

Daniel smiled, not surprised in the least.

'Fair fight,' the medicine man added. His large beaked nose gave the impression of a predatory man, yet his touch was surprisingly gentle as he rested a big hand on Daniel's shoulder. 'You are a good man. I have been to the last resting place. You bestow honour on the dead of my people.'

Daniel bowed his head slightly to acknowledge the compliment then said, 'If you wish, White Buffalo Calf, sit with us while I perform a small task.'

'I will.' He sat cross-legged beside the little fire. 'Call me Shaman – I think my English name is far too long.'

'We could just leave him out here, you know. Our job's done, like you said.' Roy was panting heavily, his arm now in a bandanna sling.

'He damn near killed me!' croaked Wes. 'This is personal!'

'What are you going to do when we get him?'

'I'll think of something. Something that'll hurt so much he'll beg me to finish him off!'

Concealed behind an outcrop, Saul tried to control his

103

breathlessness. His heart pounded and he felt dizzy with the sudden exertion. His head still throbbed; the facial cut was streaming blood. His muscles were still ridiculously stiff. He decided that all he had to do was circle back and take the three mules. All he had to do? Who was he kidding? He could barely walk. He was lucky to get this far. Maybe the best course of action would be to hide up in a cave someplace, till it was dark – couple of hours, maybe. Then steal the mules. That seemed like a good plan.

Saul slunk back into the shadows and backtracked a little.

Yes, he'd remembered all right. The cave entrance wasn't too big, but it was out of the way, mainly concealed by two pine trees that had been uprooted in heavy rainfall. He'd only noticed it earlier because he'd stumbled and grazed a shin here.

The cave opening was dark and forbidding. It might be a bear's home, he thought.

He could hear shouting further round the trail, going away, heading south. But he felt sure they'd be back. The cave was worth the risk for an hour or so. It promised succour.

'So I've promised to go back to town to help Mrs Monroe find her brother,' Daniel explained as he doused the fire with a hatful of stream water.

As the fronds of steam dissipated, he used his knife to cut round what was now an area of baked-dry mud. 'I came to fetch you, Virginia. I was worried about you.'

'With good cause, it seems,' interrupted Shaman.

Virginia managed a nod then gestured at the dried mud. 'What *are* you doing?'

He smiled up at her. 'It's just an idea – it might not work.' Carefully turning the baked mud over, his hand

104

gently brushed off soil and strands of grass. 'It's got a distinctive heel mark, see?' He pointed to a pronounced nick in the inside section of the heel imprint. 'That's quite unusual, I reckon. If we can find the boot that has that mark, we might find the culprit for all this,' he ended, waving an arm at the blackened remains of his cabin.

'Ingenious,' said Shaman, turning his face to the forest entrance. 'This man who has gone missing, is he a big man – as big as you, Daniel?'

'Aye.' His pulse raced. 'Have you seen him?'

'Yes. I note what happens in this forest and on this mountain.'

'Where is he?'

'I watched two men take their captive up the mountain.'

Daniel smiled. 'Can you take me there, Shaman?'

'Here's the hero's winnings, boss,' Drinkwater said, lowering the wads of greenbacks on O'Keefe's desk. '*Tout* last cent!'

Standing up, O'Keefe licked his lips and pulled the money towards him. Eyes alight, he said, 'Good work, Carey.' He glanced up. 'Don't worry, you'll get a bonus at the end of the week, no mistake!' He leaned over the money and started flicking through the notes, counting them.

'*Rien d'autre*, boss?'

'Come again?' O'Keefe scowled. 'Sometimes, Carey, I wish you'd speak plain English.'

'Anything else, boss?'

'Yeah, now you mention it.' O'Keefe peered at the office door, then at the vacant desk on his left. 'Don't mention this to anyone, but I want you to break into the Monroes and get me their deeds.'

'No problem, boss.'

'I'm tired of waiting for Widow Monroe to make up her mind!'

'She has too much *hauteur* – er, she's a bit full of herself, for sure, boss.'

'Whatever. If I have the deeds, I reckon I can force her out.'

'Solid plan, boss. What's Mr Smith doing, do you know?'

'Zack? Why do you ask?'

'Just rumours I picked up when I got back into town. Had me a shave and Chauncey reckons Smith has wired for a number of *bandits armés* to come into town to give him a hand.'

'Gunmen?'

'So I hear.' Drinkwater shrugged. 'It is probably only another stupid rumour. Like Smith's wanting to rename the town, you know?'

O'Keefe forced a laugh. 'Yeah, that *was* a stupid idea, wasn't it? I killed it as soon as I heard! I'm sure that Zack only wants what's best for our business.'

'Which is the Monroe depot, *hein*?'

'Right. So can you get me the deeds tonight?'

'Sure, boss. No door can keep me out, if I have a mind to get in.'

CHAPTER 9

SURE AND CERTAIN HOPE

Astride the buckboard horse, Virginia watched as Daniel put the shawl-wrapped cast of the boot-print in the left-hand saddle-bag. 'Handle that with care and keep it safe till I get back,' he said.

She nodded and stroked the cat before handing it to Shaman. The medicine man whispered something to Carson and surprisingly the cat dropped off to sleep; Shaman put him in the right-hand saddle-bag and closed the flap. 'The motion of the horse will keep him asleep,' he assured her.

Gripping Virginia's reins, Daniel looked up. 'If you can, help Ruth get legal assistance.'

'I'll try.' Her brow furrowed. 'Will you be all right?'

'I'll be OK. Tell Jonas and Ruth I intend to bring back Saul.'

She nodded and gee'd her horse into the forest, ducking branches as she went.

A few minutes later, the medicine man swung on to the back of Daniel's spare horse and the pair of them then rode along a different trail, which climbed at a steep angle.

'We have a different name for the mountain,' Shaman said. 'Where does Grimm come from?' he asked, chuckling. 'Named after those storyteller brothers, I suppose?'

'You know about the Brothers Grimm?'

'Yes, those two told very strange stories to scare children. My English teacher liked the tales so used them in my class. We do the same – but our stories were never written down. Many have been lost. Perhaps I should put them to paper before I go.'

'I reckon the world's literature would be richer for you trying, Shaman. As it happens, the brothers I'm referring to were American. But they told fairy tales right enough. There were three of them. They owned a hardware store in Bethesda Falls, apparently, when it was just a collection of tents.'

'Yes,' Shaman nodded, 'I have watched it grow.'

'Well, the three brothers spread a rumour that there was gold to be had in the mountain. As I heard it, they repeated Mark Twain's "The intestines of our mountains are gorged with precious ore to plethora." They lied – it was just a tall tale – but on the back of that they sold a *plethora* of tackle and made a pretty penny. When they'd made their money but very few found any gold, they high-tailed it out of town and were never heard of again. I don't know what its name was before, but Grimm Mountain kinda stuck after that.'

'Yes, those seeking gold came – and went. Save for you, Daniel. You found your gold.' From this vantage point on the slope, they could view the majestic peaks of the Black Hills. Shaman stared wistfully. 'I fear that in time many more white men will come and we will be powerless to stop them.'

'I hope you're wrong, Shaman.' But Daniel had seen it happen time and again. The Indians were pushed further and further west, usually with false promises. Although he was comfortable riding alongside White Buffalo Calf, he also felt like an intruder, a thief. Sure, the Sioux didn't hold with possessing things too much, and they sure as hell didn't claim any patch of land. But Daniel couldn't shake the feeling that he was transgressing, despoiling what did not belong to him. Out of the corner of Daniel's eye he admired the medicine man's proud posture and bold features, then shrugged. He reckoned it was ordained, that we must each go our own trail.

The trail led on to Front Street and Virginia was relieved to see the schoolhouse. Miss Comstock was out on the porch with a half-dozen children; she was reading to them and they listened with rapt attention. Odd, she thought, since it wasn't a school day. Then she heard the murmuring of many voices over to her right. There was a gathering up on the cemetery hill, opposite the church.

Virginia dismounted outside the school and looped the reins over the white picket-fence. She waved to Miss Comstock and the schoolteacher beckoned for her to come.

She unlatched the gate, secured it behind her and walked up the path, past forlorn but determined roses. The children sat silently watching Anna Comstock, their eyes big and round.

Virginia felt conscious of her bedraggled appearance; her make-up replaced with dirt and ash. Her auburn hair was matted, frizzy and in disarray, while her fine green dress was plucked and torn in several places, the gigot sleeves ripped, and a fair portion of the hem was badly burnt.

'Miss Simone, isn't it?' Anna Comstock said, holding out a perfectly manicured hand. Though she didn't comment, it was obvious that she had taken in Virginia's appearance.

'Yes.' Virginia brushed absently at her unkempt skirt. 'Sorry about the state I'm in, but there was a fire out at Daniel McAlister's cabin—'

'Oh, goodness! And him being such a hero in the town too – is he all right?'

'Yes, thank God.' Virginia turned on her heel and pointed to the gathering at the cemetery. 'Who's died?'

'Elliott Quincy, poor man.' Anna shielded her eyes against the sun as she studied the crowd of mourners. 'He got a good turnout, at least. Most everyone liked him. I'm looking after the children so their parents can pay their respects and offer condolences to his wife and child.'

'Yes, I remember now; I've seen him around town. What happened?'

'Some owlhoot shot him in the back while he stood guard outside the Monroe depot.' She took Virginia to one side, away from the curious eyes and ears of the children. 'Mrs Monroe has been distraught, blaming herself. I had to tell her, it was the murderer, not her. She took some convincing, I can tell you, but eventually she said she'd attend the funeral but she doesn't feel comfortable going.' Anna pursed her lips. 'For a time, Deputy Johnson arrested Mr McAlister for the murder, but you'd know that, wouldn't you? The sheriff soon put things right, though.'

'I'm glad to hear it,' Virginia said, her mind reeling. Daniel arrested? He never mentioned either the murder or the arrest. Too preoccupied with his burnt-down cabin, probably.

'I need to speak to Mrs Monroe. Can I leave my horse there?'

110

'Yes, of course. I'm sure Mrs Monroe will be glad of your company – any company.'

Saul's heavy shoulders hunched against the hard cool rock just inside the cave entrance, as if his back muscles were being absorbed into the stone. Time seemed to have no meaning. He calculated that he'd been inside over an hour, but it could have been less. He was sure he'd dozed, even though he was in an uncomfortable position.

He was surprised at how attuned his ears had become in this strange-smelling darkness. He was convinced he could hear the crawling of spiders and the scratching of ants. Maybe there were bats inside, tiny leather wings batting at the cold air, minute claws clinging to the cave ceiling. He flinched as a centipede crawled hurriedly over the back of his hand. He shook it free. So long as there were no snakes or bigger things—

'I reckon he's holed up in this here cave!'

Saul recognized the voice of Roy.

'Could be. But I ain't going in there.' Wes spoke scratchily, a symptom of his badly bruised throat and wind-pipe. 'He could brain us with a stone in the dark!'

'What'll we do?'

'Wait him out!'

'But Wes, it'll be night soon!'

'So? You ain't afeared of the dark, are you? We wait!'

Saul's heart sank. If they stayed there, he'd never be able to sneak out and steal a mule.

Time passed and eventually his stomach rumbled and he feared that his one-time abductors heard it too.

They didn't – but something else might have. . . .

From the back of the cave erupted a deep low growl and a sniffing kind of snort.

He heard the creature's feet landing heavily on loose

scree, dislodging stones, coming nearer, and Saul's blood froze.

Sheriff Latimer ticked off his list of interviewees: Pike, Anson and Wilson. Two left: the Jones family opposite the Quincy home, and the Yeslers, the neighbours of the Wilsons. He'd checked with Jim Fitzgerald and Slim's whereabouts were accounted for; Widow Quincy was now bereft of her husband's wages at the sawmill. Death's scythe cut deep and wide.

He'd even hauled in both Carey Drinkwater and Frank Gordon, but even though they were unresponsive, he could read them. Their body-language told him that they had nothing to do with Elliott's death. Sure, shiftiness flickered in their eyes for fractions of seconds – but it would not answer. They might be responsible for heinous crimes, but this wasn't one of them. He'd bet the rest of his dubious life on it. Yet even after they left his house, he felt like turning out of bed and gunning them down – for a variety of reasons, not least their disregard for decency, their arrogance and their dadblamed attitude to women in general and his Lauri in particular.

It was all so frustrating, he raged, thumping a fist on the bed's counterpane. Elliott's murderer gets away with it while the poor lad lies cold in his grave!

Of course it was possible that he was barking up the wrong tree. It wouldn't be the first time, as Lauri would be only too happy to remind him. Maybe it was one of O'Keefe or Smith's men getting a mite over-zealous. Maybe it all had to do with the owners of The Gem wanting the stage depot, after all. That begged the question, why go to all that trouble? What was so special about a stage depot? Because it was established, ripe for a takeover, that's why. What did they call it back East – a buyout.

Couldn't speak proper English, some of those banker types.

Latimer sighed and licked his lips, dearly wanting to sup a glass or two of red-eye. Good bourbon tended to stimulate the thought-processes. He considered attempting the trek out of his bedroom, along the landing and down the stairs to the drinks cabinet. He was game enough, but if his body rebelled and he collapsed, he'd suffer a tongue-lashing for weeks afterwards. And, of course, he might set back his recovery. Though he hated to admit it, sitting docilely in bed was probably the best medicine, even better than red-eye, he allowed grudgingly.

Two more interviews to go, but he'd have to wait till after the funeral. Lauri had gone, of course. He would have liked to attend, if only to study the faces of the mourners.

As Virginia walked up the path and passed between the open wrought-iron gates, she briefly recalled Bud and baby Steven. Their resting place hadn't been anywhere near as grand; in fact, it had been along the trail. She remembered staring fixedly at those two crosses among so many as she bucked and bounced in the back of the Mayos' wagon. Her vision was blurred but still she had stared, until they crested the brow of the next hill and she realized she'd seen the last of them. With the back of her hand she had wiped away her tears and consigned her husband and son to the basement of her memory – until she attended any funeral, when all too fresh remembrances were resurrected again.

Virginia sighed and was not consoled by the sight of the lugubrious Reverend John Wesley Dawson standing at the head of the open grave, his wife Rachel and their two sons by his side.

' "Out of the depths I cry to thee, O Lord!" ' The priest intoned Psalm 130 with gusto. ' "Lord, hear my voice!" '

Burying her memories, Virginia spotted Ruth Monroe on the right of the open grave and sidled over to her. Everyone was dressed either in black or dark sombre colours and Virginia suddenly felt quite conspicuous in her bedraggled green dress.

'Mrs Monroe,' Virginia whispered, gently grasping Ruth's arm.

'Oh, Miss Simone—' She gasped. 'Your face – are you all right?'

'I'll explain about me later.'

Ruth's eyes confusedly took in Virginia's disastrous dress, but her eyes quickly returned to Virginia's face, dismissing everything but her concern for her brother.

'Is Daniel . . . is he—?'

'Daniel's gone up the mountain on the trail of your brother's abductors.'

'Abductors?'

Virginia nodded and Ruth studied her, eyes showing unease; she clasped Virginia's arm and wouldn't let go. 'Thank you, Miss Simone. To know that Saul is still alive is a great boon,' she whispered and again turned her attention to the funeral service.

Virginia felt strange. As if she was no longer beyond the Pale. It wouldn't last, she knew from experience. It never did. Once her usefulness was over, she'd be dismissed again – in effect, an outcast, because of her associations and professional calling.

The preacher's long doleful face seemed appropriate for this mournful task. Virginia wouldn't particularly welcome him at a christening, though. Her heart overturned at the thought that, after all this time, she might even consider bringing into this harsh world another new defenceless life.

'Forasmuch as our brother has departed out of this life, and Almighty God in his great mercy has called him to Himself, we therefore commit his body to the ground, earth to earth, ashes to ashes, dust to dust, in sure and certain hope of the resurrection to eternal life through our Lord Jesus Christ, to whom be glory for ever and ever. . . .'

Mrs Annie Quincy stepped forward, her bowed head covered in a black lace-trimmed bonnet, and, arm trembling, she extended it over the grave and opened her fist, letting the dark soil fall onto the wooden coffin, the sound of impact dull and deadening.

Virginia's heart turned as she heard the muted crying of the little girl – Beth? – who clung tightly to her mother's skirts.

A bare-headed blond man stood to one side, his left hand on the little girl's shoulder. His steel-grey eyes stared into the grave as if it was an abyss, his long face rigid with grief.

'Who is that?' Virginia whispered.

'Reuben Anson; Elliott's best friend,' Ruth replied. 'He's been a tower of strength. I don't know how Annie would've coped with her little girl, otherwise.'

' "I heard a voice from heaven saying, 'From henceforth, blessed are the dead who die in the Lord; even so, says the Spirit; for they rest from their labours'." '

The new widow stepped back while the grave was filled in by Mike Carney and Nils Kolan, the undertaker.

Reuben rested a commiserating arm on Annie's shoulder and she sobbed. He thrust a handkerchief under her nose and she sniffled into it.

'We need to talk,' Virginia whispered.

Ruth pressed her arm. 'It will be over in a moment,' she

said, her voice heavy with grief or guilt.

Conscious of her dishevelled appearance, Virginia disengaged her arm. 'I'd better leave early, I'm not dressed appropriate. I'll get my horse and see you at the depot.'

'At the depot, yes. . . .'

As Ruth watched Virginia leave, Reverend Dawson was drawing the funeral service to a close.

'. . . one God, world without end. Amen.' Everyone mumbled 'Amen' and gradually the majority started to turn away and head back to town. A number of women went up to Annie Quincy and offered their condolences. Bravely, the new widow invited them back to her house on North Street. 'Just a small repast, you understand,' Annie said apologetically.

Ruth found herself facing Annie Quincy and for the life of her she didn't know what to say. She'd seen that same look reflected in her own mirror when Dillon lay cold seven years gone. God knows, she knew deeply what Annie was feeling, yet she couldn't put it into words or offer any solace.

Annie's mouth curled down and her eyes stared at her coldly. She turned to Reuben by her side. 'Let's get back home. We have friends to greet.'

'Aye, those who are welcome,' Reuben added. He brusquely stepped between the two women, pointedly presenting his muscular shoulder to Ruth, and took Annie's arm. In the dying embers of the setting sun the three of them strode down the path to town.

Ruth stood quite alone and felt terribly cold and it had nothing to do with the day's dying sun. She would willingly have traded places with the newly interred corpse.

CHAPTER 10

SCRATCH

Cadaverous was the best description of Chester K. Barnes, Virginia reckoned as they walked alongside him on the wooden sidewalk. He clutched his dark leather briefcase as if it contained his beating heart. Ruth had recovered from the funeral ordeal and strode purposefully alongside her.

They both pushed open The Gem saloon's batwing doors and Barnes entered ahead of them, saying, 'Thankee, ladies.' Walking up to the bar, he removed his stove-pipe hat and adjusted his dark-grey coat tails.

Virginia and Ruth hurried in and stood on either side of him.

Clearing his throat loudly, Barnes said, 'Barkeep, I'd like to speak to Mr O'Keefe right away. It's a matter of law, so don't dawdle none!'

'Right, Mr Barnes, I'll go see if he's in,' said the barkeep. He left the glistening mahogany bar and walked to the back of the room where a door proclaimed, 'Management'.

He wasn't inside long and came out rather hastily. 'You can go right in, sir, ladies.'

O'Keefe was lounging at his desk, but when he recognized Ruth Monroe, he stood up and turned on a smile. 'Mrs Monroe!'

He raised an eyebrow at Virginia. She'd washed and combed her hair, but her clothing was still abominable. Unfortunately, although Ruth had offered, none of her clothes fitted. Virginia had felt like she was wearing a tent, which was unfair, as Ruth had a good, if comely, figure. 'Miss Simone,' O'Keefe acknowledged with a smirk.

She nodded at him but kept quiet.

O'Keefe turned back to Ruth and switched on an insincere yet winning smile. 'Mrs Monroe, this *is* a timely visit!'

'That's a matter of opinion,' said Barnes.

O'Keefe glared at Barnes then eyed Ruth with a fleeting smile. 'I see you've brought a lawyer, Mrs Monroe. Don't you trust me? Isn't my offer fair?'

'Fairness has no part to play in business, Mr O'Keefe. I'm here to advise you that Mr Barnes has drawn up the preliminary agreement. Naturally, he needs you to go over it with your legal people before I – and you and Mr Zachary Smith – sign it.'

O'Keefe leaned his backside against the edge of his desk and folded his arms. 'So, you've agreed!' He smiled and Virginia thought of Carson getting some cream.

'Subject to a couple of small clauses,' Ruth said icily.

He stood up straight, moved off the desk. 'Clauses?'

'Normal for this kind of transaction, Mr O'Keefe,' offered Barnes. He pulled a sheaf of papers out of his briefcase. 'Kindly scrutinize this proposed agreement and get back to my office at your convenience.' He handed them to O'Keefe and bowed slightly. 'Ladies, shall we leave Mr O'Keefe to his reading?'

Virginia and Barnes exited the door, but at the threshold Ruth turned on her heel and said, 'Just one thing, Mr O'Keefe.'

Raising his eyes from the papers, O'Keefe said, irritably, 'What is that, Mrs Monroe?'

'If you harm a hair on my brother's head, I'll drag you through every court in the land till I get justice!' She stormed out and the door slammed shut.

O'Keefe stared, his mouth wide open. He lowered the papers to his desk. What the hell was all that about?

Saul didn't wait to find out what nightmare was coming towards him but stood up and ran. He stumbled over the higgledy-piggledy moss-covered rocks and emerged into a dusky night scene.

Roy shouted, 'There he is!'

Saul swerved to his right and lost his footing. The painful tumble, jarring his side and pelvis, probably saved his life. A bullet whanged off a nearby rock.

'Don't kill him,' Wes croaked. 'I want to do that myself, slow-like!'

'Jeezus!' Roy exclaimed as the grizzly emerged from the cave and stood bellowing on its hind legs. It spotted Saul and its nostrils twitched at his scent but it was suddenly distracted by Wes shooting. The great brown beast jerked slightly as the bullets irritated its hide. Dropping to all fours, the grizzly loped down the slope, heading straight for Wes, who emptied his Navy Colt to no avail.

Wes finally flung the empty weapon at the animal and turned and ran. But he couldn't out-race the bear. Within seconds, its great paws slashed and thudded against the man's feet and Wes, screaming for help, tumbled to the ground.

Roy fired at the great beast, his Navy Colt's slugs seeming like gnat-bites for all the notice the bear took.

Saul didn't wait to see what happened next but darted away into the trees at the bottom of the slope. Not a particularly religious man, he thanked God for his deliverance as he ran through the night-shadowed forest towards the shack.

Carrying his Henry repeater rifle, Daniel negotiated the boulders and trees till he had an uninterrupted view of the shack on the lip of the canyon. Three mules were tethered on the left. No lamplight glowed through the single window.

He glanced back. White Buffalo Calf signed 'farewell' and melted into the undergrowth. As the man said, this was white man's business. He didn't want to get involved. 'You can handle those two men,' he said with a confidence that Daniel didn't share.

His mouth dry, Daniel stepped down to the small clearing on the right of the shack.

Soundlessly, he sought the dappled shadows cast by the trees in the moonlight.

Stepping up to the window, he hunkered down and withdrew his hat. He peered through the bottom corner. The cabin was empty. It looked as though there'd been a fight, too – the table was busted and two chairs were lying on their sides.

Daniel tried the door. It wasn't locked.

Drinkwater's skeleton keys breached the lock easily enough. He used a lantern covered with a linen cloth to illuminate the office with subdued light, opening one drawer after another, careful to replace everything as he found it. When he spotted the safe in the corner, he let out a huge breath, surprised to find he'd been so tense and controlling his breathing. He knelt beside the safe and lowered the lamp. Basic, he thought, recognizing the make. He withdrew a bunch of keys and studied them, comparing each against the safe's keyhole. Two possibles, he reckoned. He tried the first; although it fitted, it didn't turn. The second did the business and he grinned with satisfaction.

He yanked on the brass handle and was about to swing the door wide when the office was brightened by an uncovered lamp. He jerked his head round and blinked, eyes trying to adjust.

Two women stood in the doorway, one of them carrying what looked like a shotgun. Stands to reason there'd be the odd scattergun around, he thought, this being a stage depot. He fleetingly shivered, as if in a cold draught, as he recognized Virginia Simone haloed by the lantern she held aloft. *Sacrebleu*, she was alive?

Disconcertingly, some mottled thing darted in front of his face and emitted a high-pitched shriek, clawing at his cheek.

Ruth Monroe said, 'I suggest you leave!'

One hand nursing his scratched cheek, Drinkwater got to his feet. 'That damned cat needs slaughtering!'

'Git, before I finish what the cat started and scratch your dad-blamed eyes out!'

'I'm gittin'!' he shouted and rushed out of the front door.

'That sure told him!' giggled Virginia as she put the lantern on the desk.

'It did, didn't it?' Ruth laughed, lowering the weapon. 'And not a French phrase passed his nasty thin lips.'

Virginia locked the safe again and removed the skeleton keys. She picked up Carson, who was licking his blood-stained claws. 'You realize the die is loaded against you?'

'Yes, I know.' Ruth walked to the front door and slammed it shut. 'Why would O'Keefe bother sending

Drinkwater round – 'specially since, for all he's aware, I've agreed to sign. He doesn't know I'm playing for time in the hope that Daniel gets back with Saul.'

Daniel swung the shack door wide open and it clattered against the wall inside. He stepped across the threshold and checked the place under the window.

Nobody – no corpse.

He was tempted to light the lantern hanging off a rafter but refrained. Instead, he uprighted a chair in the middle of the room and sat down, facing the door, his Henry ready. The sound of gunfire reached his ears but he stayed put.

Saul barged through the trees, fleeing the sound of the pursuing Roy. A shot rang out and he felt the hot stabbing pain in his left forearm. Stumbling into a tree, Saul stopped, the pain having sucked the air out of him. His big powerful legs trembled.

Roy broke through the undergrowth and aimed his Navy Colt. 'That's for wounding me, you no-account bastard!' Levelling the weapon on Saul, he added, 'Now git back to the cabin!'

'No!' Saul said, a hand on his bloody arm.

'You what?'

'If you're going to kill me, kill me *here*!'

Roy laughed. 'Kill you? Don't be stupid, I'm going to ransom you. Thanks to that bear, all the money now comes to me!' He thrust the gun barrel hard into Saul's chest. 'But if you don't do as I say, then I'll surely hurt you some more – like shooting your legs from under you! I reckon your sister'd still pay ransom for a cripple.'

Docilely, Saul moved ahead, towards the shack.

When they got there, Roy shoved Saul forward. 'Get inside!'

Saul opened the door and Roy pushed again and Saul fell through onto the floor.

'Nice evening for a stroll,' said Daniel.

'Who the hell?'

'Don't make a move, fella,' Daniel growled, 'or you're a dead man!' Without turning his head, he asked, 'Saul, are you OK?'

Saul gasped, relief in his voice. 'Yes – Daniel, is it really you?' It was dark and he recognized the voice but clearly he needed reassurance.

'Yep. Now, I think we should take this *hombre* back to town to answer a few questions, don't you?'

'Like hell you will!' Roy snarled and fired his Colt.

Seconds before the shot, Daniel gleaned the warning from Roy's words and threw himself off the chair, landing on his side. He fired the Henry as he rolled to the left. The doorjamb splintered and two more muzzle-flashes burst into the darkness and then Roy was gone.

Saul whispered, 'That's Roy – I don't know his surname. A bear got the other one, Wes.'

'OK,' said Daniel. 'Stay here. I don't aim to lose you now – your sister's quite a formidable lady and I don't want to disappoint her!'

Daniel quietly lowered the Henry to the floor and darted to the doorway.

Outside, a mule expressed its annoyance.

Standing up, Daniel drew his Colt and rushed out, running round the back of the building. Stark moonlight meant he didn't have to wait for his eyes to adjust. Dark-grey clouds scudded, obscuring thousands of stars.

Roy was trying one-handedly to mount a mule and it wasn't keen on the idea at this time of night.

'Stop!' Daniel called.

'Go to hell!' Roy twisted round and fired his six-gun.

The mule reacted instantly and moved sideways, putting all its body-weight into it, and Roy was shoved towards the lip of the chasm. He found his footing and fired in Daniel's direction again.

Instinctively, Daniel shot at Roy's feet. Dust spurted and Roy backed off, overbalanced and fell. 'Help! Jeezus, no!'

By the time Daniel reached the lip, Roy was sprawled head-first down a section of scree. He was still alive, groaning. The pistol was a few feet away. The scree seemed unsafe, emitting a low grumbling sound, liable to move at the slightest provocation.

'Help me,' croaked Roy. With a hideous rustling sound, the shale under him seemed to shift of its own accord, and he slid closer to another precipitous lip.

'For God's sake!' Roy screamed.

'Saul, bring a rope!' Daniel called.

A cloud scudded across the moon and plunged them into an eerie grey half-light.

Saul brought a lariat and Daniel cut off a length with his knife and made a lasso with it, then he looped the longer section round his waist. 'The mules are too spooked to use right now and there's no time to waste.' He eyed Saul's wounded forearm. 'Can you take our weight?'

'Aye.' Saul draped the other end of the rope over his broad shoulders. 'Go on.'

Slowly, hand over hand, Daniel gripped the rope and walked backwards over the lip and down the scree. Rather than risk dislodging more shale, he was descending to one side of Roy, mindful of the loose stones causing another rockslide.

'Please hurry!' Roy pleaded.

A couple of minutes later, he was alongside Roy. 'Here, grab this!' He dangled the short lasso over Roy, who held it tight.

'Right,' Daniel said. 'Start to sit up, slowly. I've got your weight and Saul up there's got me.'

Gingerly, Roy eased himself up in a sitting position, which wasn't easy on a downward slope.

Daniel warned, 'Don't think of trying any funny business, Roy, or I'll let go.'

Roy's Adam's apple bobbed and he nodded. Gradually, he got to his knees, then finally he stood up.

'OK, Saul!' Daniel shouted. 'Start pulling us up!'

Daniel held on to the rope with his right hand and walked forward as Saul heaved. He heard Saul growling and swearing; because of his wounded arm, the man was virtually holding on with one hand. Daniel felt as if he was being torn in two as he held Roy, no lightweight, on the other shorter rope.

Suddenly, the ground under them began moving.

Daniel shouted, 'Saul – hold tight!'

Saul stopped moving.

It was a weird sensation, like trudging through a river of mud in full spate, which threatened to tug him down, yet the river was flakes of rock and shale sliding towards the lip below. Daniel hunched his shoulders, trying to minimize the upsurge of dust into his face. Roy's rope was jerking violently but Daniel couldn't risk a glance over his shoulder since he needed to concentrate on staying upright. Dust continued to well up.

Behind them, there was a massive continuous roar as rock detritus tumbled over the edge to the dark canyon below.

Finally, the movement stopped and Daniel found that his boots were on firm stone. He breathed in a sigh of relief and immediately started coughing. He squinted backwards. Roy was spitting out gobs of dust; tears streamed down his dust-caked cheeks, but he was holding on.

'You OK, Saul?'

'Aye, I'll start pulling again!'

Sitting with his back against the cabin's outside wall, Saul gulped in air, his chest heaving with the effort.

Daniel knelt by his side and applied a length of cloth to the wound in Saul's forearm. 'At least the bullet went clean through,' he observed.

Saul nodded and continued sucking in air. The rope snaked across the ground to where Roy knelt on all fours, coughing up his lungs.

Seconds later, Roy abruptly regained his feet and flourished his Navy Colt. 'Don't make any sudden moves!' he ordered and made a hacking sound. His eyes glinted in contrast against his dust-covered face.

Daniel reckoned Roy must have retrieved the gun earlier when the clouds first obscured the moon. The damned fool risked his life for that weapon.

Roy spat on the ground. 'I'm mighty grateful you saved my life. I'd like to return the favour – *if* you let me go on my mule!'

Daniel shook his head. 'I saved you so you could bear witness against Zachary Smith. No finer reason than that, Roy.'

'Maybe so, but if you let me go, I'll let you live!'

Daniel wasn't fast on the draw. He was an accurate shot, but that was no good in a situation like this. Reluctantly, he nodded. 'Go, but—'

Before he could say another word, there was a terrifying roar on Roy's right and the trees rattled and rustled. On all fours, a grizzly bear charged out into the clearing, its snout covered in blood.

Swinging round, Roy shrieked, 'Jeezus, it just won't die!' He fired all his bullets into the beast but it just kept on rampaging towards him. Roy turned and started running towards Daniel but he was too slow. The massive paws descended on his heels and the animal dragged him down. The bear sniffed at Roy for a moment and, as if satisfied, proceeded to savage him.

'Come on,' Daniel whispered, helping Saul to his feet, 'let's hole up till Bruin's had his fill.'

Slowly, they walked sideways into the shack, Daniel with his Army Colt ready and cocked.

Once inside, Daniel lowered the beam and bolted the door. It might hold. With any luck, the grizzly would settle for its present kill. 'Those Navy Colts don't have enough stopping power; if they'd had this heavier Army model they might be alive now.'

'I'll bear that in mind in future,' Saul said, 'no pun intended.'

Daniel chuckled. 'I need to get some shut-eye. Can you keep watch?'

'Aye.' He took Daniel's Henry. 'Though I don't know how you can sleep with all that ruckus going on.'

Daniel hunkered down, his back to the wall and, ignoring the bone-crunching sounds outside, fell asleep.

Sunlight from the new day lit up the bank's big window opposite as Deputy Johnson opened the office. He went inside and put the coffee on the stove. A couple of logs soon had it heating. While he waited for the beans to brew, he leaned against the doorpost and ruminated on what Sheriff Latimer said last night. He convinced himself that he'd act on the sheriff's theory as soon as he'd drunk this coffee.

Snorting horses alerted him. Curious, he stepped outside.

Riding into town from the south were two men. Their

shadows were long and thin. Both men wore their six-guns slung low on their left hips, butts angled to the stomach.

His mouth was dry. Maybe it was the thought of the coffee? He didn't seem capable of movement as he watched the riders rein in at The Gem's hitching rail. Someone came out through the batwings to greet them. It was the stranger who'd arrived on the last stage – what was his name? Slade? That was it.

Randolph Slade now laughed out loud. 'Lee, Harley, what kept you? I've been cooling my heels waiting nigh on a week, goddammit!'

'Sorry, Randy, but we had some business of a personal nature to attend to,' Lee explained.

The replying laugh seemed to rise up from Slade's belly. 'Women are going to be the death of you one of these days!'

'But what a danged fine way to go!' chuckled Harley.

Greg Bartlett poked his head over the batwing door. 'Hey, come inside, where we can talk private!'

They strode into The Gem.

Johnson hurriedly locked the office door. He ran across the street and up the alley on the north side of the bank – First Street West, fancy name for a short passage. By the time he got to the corner of North Street, he was out of breath, and didn't see Reuben Anson until they bumped into each other.

'Sorry, Deputy,' Reuben said. 'In a hurry?'

'Yeah, I need to see the sheriff.' He noticed Mrs Quincy standing on her porch. She looked anxious then turned and slammed the door. 'Paying an early call?'

Reuben smiled. 'Oh, yeah – Annie needed my advice about some financial matters. Elliott doesn't seem to have been too careful with money.'

Johnson nodded, thinking it would be nice to have

money to worry about being careful with. 'She's lucky to have a friend like you, Reuben.'

'Oh, just being neighbourly. Besides, we've been pals for years.'

'Yeah. That reminds me. . . .'

'Yes?'

'The sheriff's calling in all rifles. Needs to do a survey. Some newfangled ordinance or something. Anyway, could you drop yours by the office at ten this morning?'

'Rifle?' Reuben shook his head. 'Sorry, Jonas, but I don't own one. I used to borrow Elliott's if I needed to do a spot of rabbit hunting.'

'OK. See you later.' Johnson hurried round the corner to the Latimer house.

Within a few minutes, he had divulged his information and fears.

'Sound like gunmen for hire, right enough,' said Latimer grimly.

'Don't even think about it!' his wife said. 'You're not fit enough to get shot up again just yet.'

'Is Mike Carney still willing to act as a deputy?'

'I reckon so, Sheriff. He was shocked by Elliott's murder, but he's keen.'

'Right.' He glanced at his wife. 'Isn't that breakfast bacon I can smell?'

'Oh, darn it!' She hurried out.

Latimer whispered, 'Keep your eyes peeled and send Carney to me with any news. I'll get out of this damned bed if I have to. Nobody shoots up my town!'

'Let's hope it don't come to that, Sheriff.'

'Hope? Yeah, we can all hope.'

CHAPTER 11

FIGHT FOR WHAT IS RIGHT

Hopes of a lucrative partnership seemed dashed now, O'Keefe thought, as he left The Gem by the back door. Why the hell had Zack hired three gunmen? As Zack didn't usually come into the office till gone midday, O'Keefe decided to go visit him instead. He couldn't remember the last time he'd been in his partner's house – a good fifteen months at least.

He passed behind the back of the jail, the courthouse and cut between the Carneys and Bodines. Smith's residence was quite out of keeping with the surrounding buildings. It had pillars, broad entrance steps, transplanted trees and bushes and two storeys of ornate balustrades. Every piece of woodwork was white. It dwarfed the homes of Mayor Pringle and the banker Eustace Hayes, Smith's most immediate neighbours.

Striding up the crazy paving and past irritating metal chimes dangling from juniper tree branches, he climbed the steps and yanked on the bell pull.

Almost immediately the door opened. 'Mr O'Keefe, sir, how can I help you?' said the smartly attired manservant.

'I'm here to see Mr Smith.' He barged past and strode into the huge vestibule with its ostentatious curving staircase directly ahead. 'I'll wait for him in the study,' he stated, and not waiting to be gainsaid, he marched to the left and swung open a door. Fortunately, his memory served him well. This was the place. He slammed the door on the manservant's squeaking expostulations.

The walls were lined with bookcases and leather-bound tomes; a writing desk was against the wall on his right, under an ornate gilt-framed painting of the Rocky Mountains.

O'Keefe was drawn to the centre of the room by an odd shape in the middle of a mahogany table. Something covered with a white linen tablecloth. He lifted a corner then hauled it off completely.

'What the hell is he up to?' O'Keefe mused.

It was a miniature model of the town – with several additional buildings, each of which sported a label on a tiny flagpole: *Zachary Smith's*. Then O'Keefe was drawn to the display's plaque: *Smithville*.

'I see you've discovered my little secret.' Smith's resonant voice didn't seem annoyed.

Whirling round, O'Keefe said, 'Well, it's not a complete surprise, though I thought you'd dropped the idea.'

Smith closed the door behind him soundlessly. He thrust his hands deep into the pockets of his dark-red dressing gown and smiled, though his tobacco-stained teeth suggested a grimace more than mirth. 'I have plans. The Gem and the livery stable are just the beginning. I actually have an offer on the hotel and the general store, as well as the stage depot.'

Turning to study the diorama, O'Keefe whistled. 'You're sandwiching in certain businesses – you're going to squeeze them out.'

'They'll be glad to take my terms. Better to work for me – and my town – than to push up daisies, eh?'

O'Keefe's blood ran cold. He had his ruthless moments; he applied force when it suited, but this was in a different league entirely. 'Your hired gunmen. Are they part of the plan?'

'Most decidedly. Once I set them on Mrs Monroe, the rest will fall into line. . . .'

Trying to seem nonchalant, O'Keefe stuck his thumbs in his vest pockets. Through the material his fingers felt the comforting bulge of the derringer. 'Did you have anything to do with the disappearance of her brother?'

Smith chuckled, his fierce eyes alight. 'I thought it would soften her up. Yesterday's legal visit convinced me she was bluffing, hoping that by some miracle her beloved brother would return in one piece!' He withdrew his hands and cracked his knuckles. 'Silly woman!'

'Yeah, as you say. . . .'

'Are you comfortable with my plans, Royce?' There was a crazed look in Smith's eyes now and the veins at his neck stood out in livid ridges. 'I need to know.'

Nodding rather too much, O'Keefe said, 'The Gem's success is our success, Zack. If you're going to take over the town, then I'd like some of the action.' He offered a smile and hoped that it appeared genuine.

'That's a gambling man talking!' He slapped O'Keefe on the back and shepherded him to the door.

'Sorry to disturb you this early. I just wanted those gunmen clarified, that's all.'

'I understand, Royce. Have no fear, I'll take you with me – Bethesda Falls may become Smithville in time, but you can be assured of being my right-hand man. My lieutenant. There's enough power to go round; it'll reside with both of us. Good God, I'm only forty-eight – we've got years to fulfil this dream! And we will, partner.'

Grinning from ear to ear, O'Keefe said, 'It sounds good

to me, Zack.' Inwardly, he cringed from his partner's cling-ing touch.

When he was outside and the front door shut, he let out a long thin sigh. Shakily he took off his hat and wiped his forehead with a handkerchief, forcing himself not to run. Replacing his hat, he passed Kolan's carpenter's shop and the Gallagher family home and came out into Main Street.

Smith was clearly mad and must be stopped.

Riding into town from the north were two men and O'Keefe recognized them. Saul Barchus, his arm in a sling, rode a mule and Daniel McAlister was astride his chestnut; two mules trailed behind. Surprisingly, a wave of relief washed over him as he realized that Zack's abduc-tion ploy had failed. He was tempted to run up and tell them what he'd just witnessed, but he didn't reckon on getting much sympathy there. Maybe the answer was to get out of town – until the gunfighters had gone. He blanched at the potential damage they could cause.

Against his better judgement, O'Keefe strode down the boardwalk to his saloon. Take down the paintings and mirrors, at least. Remove the bottles from the shelves. Windows were always a risk in a saloon.

He paused at the sheriff's office. ' 'Morning, Mike.'

'Good morning, Mr O'Keefe,' Carney said, rising from the chair.

'Good news about Mrs Monroe's brother, isn't it?' O'Keefe said, gesturing at the two riders who were dismounting outside the stage depot.

'Yeah, I reckon she'll be glad he came to no real harm.'

O'Keefe concealed a shudder. An arm in a sling signi-fied real harm to him. 'Is Deputy Johnson in?'

'Nope, he's visiting Mrs Monroe.'

'My sympathies lie with you, Mrs Monroe,' Deputy

Johnson said, dry-wringing his hands in the depot office. 'But I have to warn you that the course of action you're taking is foolhardy.'

'Whatever my sister does is OK with me,' said Saul Barchus, filling the doorway.

Ruth turned and stared. 'Saul, you're safe!' Lifting her skirts, she rushed up to him. Then she noticed his sling and the reopened wound on his face. 'You're hurt!'

Virginia let out a squeal of delight and ran to embrace Daniel.

'Well, I guess everything's all right now then,' mumbled Jonas.

Ruth rested a hand on her brother's bandaged arm and turned. 'No, Deputy, we still aim to go down there. You can either come with us or leave town. I don't reckon you'll go against us, though.'

Saul eyed her. 'What's going on, Sis?'

'At least four gunmen are in The Gem, probably waiting for the order to come down here to shoot us up,' Ruth explained. 'Virginia and me have decided to take the fight to them!'

Daniel stared down at Virginia. 'Is this true?'

She nodded. 'We won't be bullied. Mrs Monroe – Ruth – she's worked damned hard to build up this business. She doesn't want some power-hungry ignoramus taking it away from her.'

'Well said, ma'am!'

All eyes were drawn to the doorway again.

'Horace Q. Marcy.' He bowed slightly. 'I concur with your sentiment. I believe your depot is worth fighting for, ma'am,' he said, addressing Ruth. 'I'm willing to join you, if you'll have me.'

'This is absolute madness!' railed Deputy Johnson, making his way to the door. He edged past Marcy then

134

hesitated on the threshold, staring at all of them. He returned his gaze to Ruth Monroe. She stared right back. 'Oh, hell, I'll come with you – maybe I can talk some sense into those gunmen before any harm is done.'

'Thank you, Jonas,' Ruth said, 'but why are you doing this?'

'I'm . . . because . . . I—' His wide-set, dun coloured eyes shifted left and right. 'B – Because it's the right thing to do, ma'am,' Jonas said finally. His cheeks were red.

Once they'd finished laying out the weapons on the desk, Daniel helped Ruth tether and hobble the horses in the corral. If there was any shooting, she didn't want them distressed.

As they walked to the depot's rear entrance, Daniel said, 'Are you sure you want to do this?' He stopped and held her arms. 'When the lead flies, things happen darned fast. Sometimes, folk don't even know who they're shooting at. It's an awful mess.'

'I've used a shotgun in anger, Daniel. There's many a time when I've had to replace a drunken shotgun rider so we could get the stage through.'

'I'm sure you can handle yourself, it's just – I'm not overly happy about you two ladies being armed and fighting gunmen.'

She gripped his arm tightly. 'Virginia told me what happened up at your place. It's that kind of mentality we're fighting today, Daniel. People who are so arrogant they think they can walk over anybody they see fit. They don't give a damn!' Her eyes filled with tears but she blinked them away. 'If I can't fight for what is right and what I believe in – especially after so many have done in our terrible Civil War – then I don't reckon I can ever look at myself in the mirror again.'

'You're very brave to do this.'

'Jonas says I'm foolhardy.'

'He's just concerned for your safety.'

'I'm afraid, actually. I feel awful about poor Elliott being murdered because of me. And now all of you are taking my side. When it's my fight – not yours, not Virginia's.'

'You realize that Jonas is staying because he has an unspoken affection for you?'

'Jonas?' She flushed. 'Me?' Her hand went up to her scarred mouth.

'Yes, you, Ruth.'

'Let's get back. The others will be worrying, wondering where we've got to.'

Deputy Jonas Johnson watched them nervously. He wanted to be anywhere but here right now. He'd fired his Navy Colt in the line of duty three times, but on each occasion he'd been with Sheriff Latimer so he was never sure if any of his few shots hit their mark. He hated the smell of gunsmoke but he was reassured by Saul's presence.

Saul was handed a shotgun by Ruth; hers was by her side on the desk. 'I know you don't like guns, Saul, but we – *I* – need your help in this.'

'Don't worry, Sis, I'll do my bit. What's it loaded with?'

'Double-O buckshot. You have to get up close for it to be lethal, if that's any comfort.'

'Some. I'm not keen on killing anybody, no matter how bad they are.' He manipulated the stock against his shoulder and tested it for weight. He winced a little, probably as he was reminded of his wounded forearm. 'Aye, I can handle this OK.'

If Saul could overcome his distaste of weapons then, Jonas reasoned, he'd better do the same. He glanced over at the others.

Marcy wore a Remington Army .44 in a dark leather holster strapped to his thigh: 'I heard that it's superior to the Colt,' Marcy remarked.

'Haven't you compared them?' Daniel asked, checking the spare cylinder of his Army Colt.

'No. If someone has written that appraisal, I'm liable to believe it.'

Daniel's eyes widened in surprise. 'You believe everything you read in the newspapers?'

'Well, of course not! Advertisers tend to exaggerate and I reckon that Mark Twain's a teller of tall stories. In fact, I'm sure most of his fellow journalists have similar mendacious ink in their veins.'

'Yeah, right,' Daniel said.

Jonas scratched his head. Easterners!

Virginia emptied a box of .44 shells into her hand and put them in her skirt pocket. Then she hefted the Henry and loaded sixteen. 'Will they be expecting us, do you think?'

'Probably,' replied Daniel. He eyed Jonas. 'Are you happy with our formation?'

Jonas swallowed and nodded. Then he cleared his throat, mindful of Ruth's eyes on him. 'Yes. I'll go a couple of paces ahead. Gives me a chance to talk some sense into those guys.'

CHAPTER 12

'A MITE BRUTISH'

Hands clammy and his mouth and throat dry, Jonas stepped out with Saul a couple of paces behind him. It was a hot afternoon and there were no shadows, just a stark empty street. They walked into the middle of the road.

'It looks like they're expecting us,' Saul observed.

Not a soul stirred.

Next, Marcy came out, followed by Ruth. They crossed the street in a diagonal direction, stepping up on to the boardwalk outside The Constitution Hotel.

Daniel and Virginia walked out. Daniel shut the stage depot door behind them. They stayed on their side of the thoroughfare and took measured strides along the board-walk, past Pike's Grocery Store.

Daniel paused at the boardwalk's down-steps by the entrance to an alley that ran along the side of Powers' Drug Store; his eagle eye had caught movement at the north end of town. 'Steady, Virginia,' he whispered, advising caution with an outstretched left arm. He whistled across to Marcy and nodded ahead.

Marcy stopped walking and stood with Ruth outside the barber-shop.

'That's Zachary Smith!' Virginia said.

'You're sure?'

'Yes, that's definitely him. I don't recognize the guy in the back of the wagon.'

Sitting on his buckboard seat, Smith was dressed in black, his hat on the back of his head. A cigar was clamped between his grinning teeth. The two black horses, complete with black feather plumes, suggested that they'd absconded from their chore of pulling a hearse.

'That's Randolph Slade with Smith!' Jonas called over.

'What's Smith up to?' Marcy shouted.

'Let's go and find out!' Jonas responded.

They all started walking up town again.

And the buckboard approached, the horses moving sedately, as if in a funeral cortège.

Passing the drug store, Jonas stopped level with the entrance of the saloon. He had detected no movement down the alley that ran along the side of the The Gem. He held up a slightly shaky hand to Zachary Smith. 'Mr Smith, sir! I'd appreciate it if you'd step down and have a civil word.'

The buckboard passed the sheriff's office and halted in front of the cobbler's.

Mike Carney stood at the office door, his hand hovering anxiously over his holstered pistol.

Smith smiled maliciously. 'What have we got to talk about, Deputy?'

'I reckon things are about to get out of hand, sir. With a little reasonableness on each side, we could avoid a lot of bloodshed.'

'Tell that to Mrs Monroe over there!' he ground out, between cigar and clenched teeth. 'She's heading my way with a deadly weapon. I don't call that reasonable, Deputy!'

Saul was a pace behind Jonas and now slowly moved a couple of feet to the right, which afforded him a better view of Slade in the back of the buckboard; he kept the cocked shotgun in the crook of his arm, pointing down.

Smith seemed to scan beyond Jonas and the others, towards the southern end of town. A flash of irritation darkened his features.

Jonas glanced over his shoulder and grinned. Townspeople were emerging from The Constitution Hotel, the grocery store, the El Dorado and the drug store. Carrying rifles and shotguns, the men were to the front, spanning across the street – Chauncey, the barber, Jack Perry, Edward Pike, Spence Chapman . . . Behind them clustered women, many of them holding placards that proclaimed: 'We won't sell!' and 'Leave our town alone!'

Standing up, Smith looped the reins over the wagon's foot-rail and glared at the crowd. 'They've got no idea! Progress means moving on! *I'm* their future, damn them!'

'Sir,' Jonas persisted, his face glistening with sweat, 'your methods of business, they're a mite brutish.'

'Brutish? Ye Gods, we're trying to tame the West and you worry about my business methods?' He swore.

'No need to get your dander up, Mr Smith, I'm only doing my job, which means keeping the peace.'

Smith took the cigar from his mouth and expelled a blue cloud of smoke. 'Peace? We all get that, eventually. Perpetual peace. I'm not ready yet.' Replacing the cigar, he cracked his knuckles.

Jonas had seen Smith perform that irritating action on many occasions. But some odd instinct warned him that this time it was a signal. He whirled round and started running to the left. 'Get to cover!'

Everything happened fast.

Slade shot Mike Carney outside the sheriff's office

before the young man could clear leather.

As Carney stumbled to the boardwalk, toppling a chair, Saul stood his ground and blasted the shotgun at Slade. But one of the horses had reacted to Slade's shots and shimmied sideways and took Saul's shotgun blast full in the head. Shrieking loudly, the bloodied animal toppled to the right into its partner, the traces jangling.

The buckboard jerked and half-overturned.

Zachary Smith and Slade jumped clear and landed firmly on the ground. Smith darted back up the street towards the courthouse and the West Second Street alley. Slade's boots pounded on the wooden boards outside the cobbler's next door to the sheriff's office. He forced the door easily and lurched inside, reloading as he went.

When Slade fired, Harley and Lee emerged from their hiding place round the general store's corner. They were met by a fusillade of lead from Marcy and Jonas. Marcy's bullets disarmed Harley. 'Shit!' exclaimed Harley, gripping a wounded arm.

'Get down!' Ruth ordered.

Both Marcy and Jonas dropped to their knees as Ruth fired the shotgun.

Several balls slammed viciously into Lee. The man's chest mushroomed into a welter of dark red spots. He was dead before he hit the ground.

'Jeezus!' Harley's leg had been hit by shot too. Gasping for breath, he scrambled behind the brick wall of the store.

When Slade fired, Frank and Greg ran out of The Gem fanning their revolvers, delivering a lot of lead, but there was no accuracy behind it.

A slug plucked at Saul's shoulder and he sank to his

knees to fumble a reload.

Daniel heard several bullets whiz past his ear. His heart lurched, fearing for Virginia, but in the same instant he aimed, arm rock-steady, and fired his Army Colt, his two bullets pounding into Frank Gordon's belly.

Gordon stumbled into Greg and both their weapons discharged harmlessly, shattering the saloon glass window.

Greg fell through the window into the saloon while Gordon curled up on the boardwalk, whimpering in agony.

Barely five seconds had elapsed. Acrid black powder gunsmoke drifted and an eerie stillness descended. Snorting, the surviving black horse shied away from its dead partner. There was no sign of the protesting towns-people; they'd run to either side of the street, away from the hot lead.

'Saul, you're hurt!' Ruth exclaimed, all set to run to him.

'Stay there, Sis! I'm fine.' He stood up unsteadily and peered towards the south end of town. 'Where are Drinkwater and O'Keefe?'

'Maybe it isn't their fight,' suggested Virginia. 'O'Keefe may be crooked, but he's no killer.'

'I'm *almost* flattered to hear you say that, Virginia Simone,' O'Keefe said, pushing open the saloon's batwing doors. He shook his head as weapons were trained on him. 'Nope, I'm not armed. Just a spectator.' He thumbed over his shoulder. 'Greg ran upstairs. God knows why.'

'Maybe he's hoping to enter Heaven on Earth before he dies,' Daniel suggested.

'Have you any girls upstairs?' Virginia demanded.

'Two – Colleen and Mabel. Why?'

'He might use them as hostages,' she said, striding to

142

the swing-doors.

O'Keefe eyed the broken window. 'Have a care with the furniture when you go after him.'

But Daniel's hand grabbed Virginia's shoulder. 'No, we don't rush in anywhere,' he said.

She nodded, her lips a tight determined line, and reluctantly moved against the wall at the side of the saloon entrance.

Ominous metallic sounds, as weapons were reloaded, cut through the whimpering of Gordon and the whickering of the surviving buckboard horse.

'Take stock,' Daniel urged quietly. 'Saul, are you fit enough?'

'Yeah, I'll do.' He walked over to Lee's body and took the man's handgun; fingers shaking, he reloaded from the dead man's belt. 'I'll keep an eye out for Drinkwater.' He rubbed his cut face. 'I owe him.'

'Right, but save some of him for me. Jonas. Did you see where Smith went?'

'Headed for the courthouse. Probably gone home. Slade went into the cobbler's—'

'I'll take Harley,' said Marcy. 'He went this way,' he signed to his left. Pale-faced, Ruth followed him.

'Don't try anything foolish,' Daniel said. 'We were lucky this time. We mightn't be again.'

'Oh, I reckon you're naturally lucky,' Jonas said.

'Could be. Jonas, leave Slade to me – you go after Greg.' Jonas stared, unsure.

'I've killed before. Slade's a killer and won't hesitate.' Jonas swallowed. 'OK, Daniel. But be careful.'

Daniel turned to Virginia. 'Leave it to Jonas. I don't want to lose you now.'

'You be careful too,' she said and watched him go.

Hugging the wooden walls of the saloon, Daniel hurried to the end of the boardwalk and peered round the corner. The cobbler's window was closed and there was nobody in the alley. He crossed the space and rushed up the steps to the walkway outside the cobbler's. The front door was ajar. On the other side of the door was a window with several shoes on display.

Daniel hunkered down and pushed the door wide, his Colt steady. There was no movement inside. He sprang through and darted to the right and shoulder-barged a rack of boots. As he steadied it, a shot rang out, splintering the wooden wall behind him. Opposite was a counter and behind that a workbench. There was a strong smell of leather. To the far left was a staircase, probably leading to living quarters. Was the cobbler on the premises, would he come down to investigate – or stay out of the way?

Light percolated through the front and side windows. Recently disturbed dust danced in a sunbeam. The shot had come from the left.

Another shot now, from behind the counter, thwacking into a boot behind to his left.

'Hey, Slade, if you're such a good gunman, why are you hiding behind a serving counter? Is your courage so small, you have to shoehorn it into a child's boot?'

Two more shots. The movement was by the money till; he was shooting blind.

Daniel stood up and fired four shots, bouncing them off the surface of the counter, and they ricocheted. He heard a gasp and a cut-short yelp.

Seconds later, Slade appeared at the right-hand end of the counter. He threw a heavy metal last, his aim surprisingly good – or lucky. Maybe Daniel's luck had run out, after all. An edge of the last hit Daniel's forearm, the pain excruciating, and he dropped his weapon just as Slade

144

bundled into him.

Slade was a big man and fast with his fists. There was a lot of blood; Daniel realized that some of it came from Slade – a lucky ricochet had severed two fingers on the man's gun-hand.

That was of little comfort as Slade straddled him now, legs pinioning Daniel's arms to the floor. Slade's eyes gleamed, even the lazy one, as he grabbed the metal last and raised it above his head, intent on braining Daniel.

CHAPTER 13

STAINED A FEARFUL RED

The front window shattered into fragments. Slade's chest fountained blood from two gaping wounds and he was instantaneously thrust off Daniel, back into the shop. Slade slumped to the floor and fell on his side, the heavy last dropping from lifeless hands and pounding into his lazy eye, nose and mouth, though he was beyond caring.

Daniel sat up.

Virginia stood outside the shattered window, the Henry barrel smoking.

Eyeing Slade's corpse, Daniel said, 'I guess he's breathed his last.'

Jonas strode past O'Keefe. 'Upstairs, you said?'

'Yeah. Be my guest.'

As Jonas climbed the staircase cautiously, his gun ready, O'Keefe hurried to the back door of the saloon and left.

Halfway up the stairs, Jonas ducked, showered by wood splinters as the balusters were shattered from a flurry of shots. Fearfully, he fired back.

'Don't shoot again, lawman, or you'll kill an innocent girl!'

Jonas stopped shooting as Greg appeared on the landing behind Mabel, who was sobbing. He had her arm up her back and she seemed frozen with fear. Greg sneered. 'I aim to come down them stairs, Deputy, and you'll wave me off on a horse.' He fired a single shot and a newel post splintered beside Jonas. 'When we get out of town, I'll let the pretty lass go.'

God, I'm trapped, Jonas thought. Angry that his life should come to this sorry end, he slowly stood tall and straightened his gun-arm. 'I ain't moving, Greg! I might die, but you're going with me! Now let Miss Mabel go!'

'Her name's Mabel, is it?' Greg thumbed back the trigger of his six-gun and pressed the muzzle to Mabel's head. 'You shoot and she has that name on a tombstone!' Mabel's eyes were tight shut, lips trembling.

Abruptly, two loud shots echoed behind Jonas and in almost the same instant Greg twisted round, half his face blown away. Mabel broke free from Greg's grip and fell to her knees on the landing as Greg stumbled to the banister rail and burst through, toppling head-first on to a round table below.

Glancing back, his gun smoking, Jonas saw Sheriff Latimer leaning against the batwing door; he was wearing pants but his chest and shoulders were still bandaged. 'I said that you had sand, Deputy.' Latimer smiled a crooked grimace.

Marcy didn't have to track the fleeing Harley far. Ruth's shotgun slugs had severed an artery in the man's leg. He lay dying against the Yesler household's white picket fence, the wood stained a fearful red.

A pace behind, Ruth stopped in her tracks. 'Oh, my

God,' she moaned and stumbled to a strip of wasteland and disgorged her stomach's contents.

When O'Keefe got to Zachary Smith's house, he found that the front door was open. Inside, he passed the servant's body, the man's head a bloody mess, as if he'd been battered in a frenzied attack. O'Keefe noticed that the study doors were open and he could hear muted sobbing.

Gingerly, he crossed the hallway and, his body tense, he stood in the doorway and surveyed the room.

With his back to the door, Zachary Smith was leaning over the Smithville model, his blood-stained hands gripping the edge of the mahogany table. He was whimpering, his shoulders shaking.

'It seems that the town isn't too keen on your vision for them, Zack.'

Zachary Smith swung round, eyes blazing. 'Where were you? You were supposed to hit them from the south!'

O'Keefe smiled. 'You must be mistaken. I never promised you anything.' He tucked his thumbs in his vest pockets. 'I recall saying I liked the idea of having more power.'

'You could have had much more, if you'd backed me!'

O'Keefe shook his head. 'No, Zack. You've never been a true gambler. You don't understand people. They'd have resented your vision. Really.'

Smith seemed to pull himself together and walked rather hesitantly to the desk. He flicked a lever and the framed Rocky Mountain picture swung away from the wall to reveal a safe.

O'Keefe said, 'Zack, I think it might be best if you leave town.'

Manipulating the combination, Smith said, 'Yeah, that's

148

it. I'll go away for a while.' The safe door clicked and he swung it open. Smith lifted a briefcase from the knee-well and placed it on the desk.

'Actually, Zach, I thought you should go away for good.'

One hand resting on the safe's shelf, Smith faced him. 'What?'

'Forever, in fact.' O'Keefe smoothly withdrew his derringer, extended his arm and fired. His aim was deadly accurate and the .44 bullet penetrated Smith's right eye.

Smith jerked and his body went into a shocking spasm. He dropped to the desk top then to the carpet.

Calmly walking over to the safe, O'Keefe carefully folded Smith's limp hand round the empty derringer. Few would argue that it wasn't suicide. The embarrassment of the model of Smithville – and his murdered servant – would be evidence enough for any investigation. Now he pulled out all the money, deeds and other papers, cramming them in the briefcase. He slammed the safe shut, twirled the combination wheel and clicked the painting back in place.

O'Keefe smiled and left without a backward glance.

O'Keefe entered The Gem. The barkeep was sweeping up glass and a waitress was mopping an unpleasant red smear on the floorboards beneath the busted staircase. O'Keefe was relieved to note that any bodies had been removed. Suddenly his grip on the briefcase tightened. Carey Drinkwater sat at a table in the rear, his feet up.

'Are you waiting for me?' O'Keefe asked.

'No, boss. I reckon I'll be having a visit from our hero fellow shortly.' He grinned and eyed the Colt .44 concealed under the table.

'Well, don't make too much mess,' he said, heading for his office. 'It all costs money, you know.'

'Sure, boss.'

Once inside his office, O'Keefe breathed a sigh of relief. He clutched the briefcase to his chest. He needed a drink. Lowering the briefcase to his desk, he crossed over to the drinks cabinet and poured a good measure of brandy. Then he'd get the contents of the briefcase into the safe.

He sipped, savouring the fiery taste and almost spluttered as there was a knock on the door.

'Who is it?'

'Virginia Simone, Mr O'Keefe.'

Come back to plead for her job? Well, she was damned good at it, he allowed. Maybe she had a couple more seasons left in her before being replaced by someone younger and prettier. 'Come in!'

She walked in and he thought that she looked an absolute mess. He was considering a reassessment of her prospective employment when she stopped at the chair in front of his desk and rested a booted foot on it. Her dress fell away to expose leg up to her alabaster thigh.

He smiled and held up his tumbler. 'Drink?'

'That would be nice.'

Turning his back on her, he found a glass and poured a good measure. Not bad, those legs. Maybe he should get her to wear a waitress outfit at the wheel. He replaced the decanter's glass stopper.

She smiled at him as he moved away from the cabinet and handed her the glass. As their fingers touched he felt a slight frisson. 'Have you come back for your job? It's available, if you want it.'

She shook her head. 'No, I just needed to pass the time while Daniel conducts some unfinished business with Drinkwater.'

'Oh.' He was annoyed to find that he couldn't avoid his

disappointment in that single word.

She smiled sweetly. 'Shall we sit for a few minutes?'

'I think you might want to prepare yourself for a bad outcome—'

'Want to bet on it?'

'I bet you didn't expect to find me here, did you, hero?' Drinkwater had sneered as Daniel and Virginia had entered the saloon.

Daniel carried a parcel in his left hand and, with his right, cocked his hat to the back of his head. 'No, I'm surprised. But pleased all the same. Saves me having to hunt you down.'

'He's awful considerate at times, is our Drinkwater,' Virginia said, then pursed her lips in thought. 'No, *scratch* that comment. . . .'

The cat's scratch-marks on Drinkwater's cheek seemed to redden as he glared at her.

'Haven't you got business with O'Keefe?' Daniel asked.

She nodded then eyed Drinkwater. 'Is it all right if I go in to see Mr O'Keefe?'

'Sure.' Drinkwater leered. 'You might want to beg for your job.'

'All things are possible,' she said, and moved to the back office and knocked.

After she went inside and closed the door, Daniel said, 'An excellent pair of boots you've got there.'

'*Mai oui*, finest tooled leather. You want a pair? It could be arranged for you to be buried in them.'

'No, too fancy for my taste. Interesting design etched into the heel.' Daniel heard the faintest click of a gun-hammer being pulled back.

CHAPTER 14

STRAIN THE WALLS

At that moment, Deputy Johnson strode into the bar. 'I'd think carefully about your next move, Mr Drinkwater.'

Careful not to block Johnson's aim or view, Daniel unwrapped the parcel. It was the mud-cast he'd made. 'This is evidence that you were at the scene of my cabin's fire. You burned it down and stole my gold and winnings.'

The colour drained from Drinkwater's face.

Deputy Johnson stood next to them now. 'It's as good as a witness, Mr Drinkwater.' He rested his hand on the walnut grip of his holstered pistol. 'Are you going to come peacefully or do we get to have more gunplay?'

Drinkwater lowered his eyes and slowly uncocked the weapon and raised his hands, careful to lift the Colt without implying any threat.

'Very sensible,' Daniel said though there was a note of regret in his tone. 'And, of course, the deputy here will search your room. I'd like to think you kept my gold safe for me.'

Drinkwater scowled.

'*Touché*'s the word you're looking for,' suggested Daniel.

It was quite a gathering in Sheriff Latimer's bedroom. Lauri sat on the bed and remarked, 'If we tried to get any more in here, we'd strain the walls.'

'Yes. But it's necessary to bring my investigation to a conclusion.'

She sighed. 'Do as you wish, dear. You usually do.'

Jonas and Horace Q. Marcy stood sheepishly by the door during this marital exchange.

Standing around the bed were Reuben Anson, Slim Wilson and Eddie Pike.

'Eddie, I want to talk to you first.'

'Sheriff?'

'You owed Elliott big time. He lent you money when you had cash-flow problems. You never repaid him.'

'Who says?'

'Eustace Hayes, your bank manager.'

His face purpling, Pike said, 'He has no right to divulge my private finances!'

'This is a murder enquiry, Eddie. I have every right. I'm the law around here, and don't you forget it!'

'But I didn't kill Elliott!'

'You can wait on the landing. Stay with him, Jonas.'

Pike and Jonas left the room.

'I'd be a little worried, if I was you,' said his wife to the other two. 'He's only got started.'

Slim Wilson swallowed and glanced at the window. It was too small an escape route for his big body.

'As for you, Slim, I know that you resented Elliott because he had money while you had to scrimp and save. During your boozy nights, he often paid more than his fair share and you let him – but you resented it.'

153

'I did not! He was my pal!'

'The barkeep told me different when I visited The Gem after the shootout with Greg.'

Lauri made a disapproving sound in her throat.

Slim appeared cowed.

Latimer said, 'Wait outside.'

Slim Wilson left and Latimer said, 'Mr Marcy, please show in Mrs Quincy and her daughter, Beth.'

Her daughter in front of her, Annie Quincy entered and eyed Marcy, Reuben, Mrs Latimer and the sheriff. 'Sheriff,' she acknowledged.

'Ma'am,' he said. 'I'm sorry to involve you and your lovely daughter in my investigations but I assure you that it's necessary.'

She nodded and lowered her gaze, gently placing a hand on her daughter's head.

'As it happens,' Latimer said, 'Cecil's been a mite busy at the telegraph office.'

Annie looked up and seemed puzzled.

'I checked with your home town in Iowa – Cedar Falls, wasn't it?'

'Yes,' she croaked and glanced away.

'Luckily, the sheriff there knows his townspeople. He remembers all three of you. Annie, you were betrothed to Reuben then Elliott came into a big inheritance and all of a sudden you gave Reuben the mitten and eloped with Elliott. Is that right?'

She shook her head, eyes awash. 'It wasn't like that. You make it sound cold and calculated. I just fell in love with Elliott.' Her daughter squirmed under her tightening grip. 'We left because we didn't want to hurt Reuben, him seeing us together every day an' all.'

Latimer nodded. 'Just so. Not long after you married you gave birth to Beth here; a few months later, you came

154

to Bethesda Falls and Elliott had your present home built. Right?'

Beth tugged at her mother's hand. 'Mummy, I don't understand – last night you said Reuben was my real Daddy, not Elliott. . . .'

A palpable silence fell on the room.

Reuben drew his revolver and backed to the door. But Marcy was quick, the butt of his gun slamming into the back of Reuben's skull. Crumpling under the blow, Reuben fell unconscious to the floor.

Annie screamed and Beth started crying. Mrs Latimer went over to comfort the little girl. 'Sheriff, I reckon you've got your killer,' said Marcy.

'I sure have. You know, that telegraph office is a valuable asset in the fight against crime.'

'It certainly is,' Marcy said and smiled.

'And I think you have some unfinished business with my deputy?'

'Is it OK to leave you?' He eyed Mrs Quincy and the comatose Reuben.

'Just take his gun with you. I'm sure Mrs Latimer can handle everything, can't you, dear?'

'Aye, Henry. I'm forever clearing up your mess. Why should today be any different?'

When O'Keefe was alone, he returned the two tumblers to the drinks cabinet. Then he opened the safe and turned to the briefcase. He snapped it wide and stared. The papers were there but instead of money there was a bottle of whiskey. How the hell. . . ?

Sleight-of-hand? It wasn't possible! She must have hidden the bottle under her skirt – falling open like that, it made it easy to get the bottle out – while his back was turned, while he poured her drink. Jeezus, she must have moved *fast* – shoving the money in the same concealed pocket she'd hidden the bottle.

And legally there wasn't a damned thing he could do about it.

He remembered the money McAlister won and Drinkwater had brought back. It amounted to not much less than he'd stolen from Smith's safe. He shrugged philosophically. It wasn't his money, it was Smith's; he was no worse off, he supposed. He turned the name-plaque *Mr Zachary Smith* face down on the empty desk. In fact, he was sole owner of The Gem, his poor partner deceased.

O'Keefe moved back to the drinks cabinet and smiled. He poured another brandy. Virginia Simone was good. Really good. He hoped that McAlister appreciated her.

Virginia's original plan had been to knock out O'Keefe with the whiskey bottle. Then she'd use Drinkwater's skeleton keys on the safe. But a hasty opportunist look inside the briefcase altered her scheme. She simply switched the whiskey for the money in mere seconds.

Wally Egan reined in his roan outside the Guthrie Staging Post. As he dismounted, a man appeared in the doorway of the adjacent stable building. He stood beside his pinto and behind them was a pack mule.

'Hey, Pete, are you all set?' Wally asked.

Pete was a pinch-faced, thin individual; he nodded and tugged at the reins of his piebald horse. 'About time you got here!'

'You got my telegram?'

'Yeah, but I still don't see why you had to hang around so long!'

'I wanted to make sure old Alf was OK.'

Pete scowled. 'Well, you shouldn't have shot him!'

'I had no choice, he'd pulled the scattergun on me!'

Pete sighed and mounted up. 'Look, Wally, we need to get out now. Have you brung the loot?'

'Yeah, I stopped at the hiding place on the way.' He slapped his bulging saddle-bags.

'That's what I wanted to hear!' a voice barked from the side of the stables.

Turning in his saddle, Pete said, 'Who the hell are you, mister?'

'Jeezus,' Wally exclaimed, recognizing Marcy, 'he was on the coach!' Wally grabbed the reins and cantle and shoved a foot into a stirrup.

'Don't make another move!' Deputy Johnson warned as he emerged from the other side of the stable building. He sat astride his horse, rifle covering both Wally and Pete.

'What's going on here, Wally?' Pete wanted to know.

'Step down from your horse, mister!' Marcy ordered, resting his revolver on his pommel.

'I'd do as the agent says,' warned Jonas. 'He's a fine shot.'

'Agent?' squeaked Pete.

'Step down!'

Finally, Pete dismounted, his face clouded. His eyes switched from Marcy to the deputy and back to Wally.

'Don't think about escaping,' Marcy said. 'You're wanted dead or alive, Pete Quinn, so I can take you back quick or dead. Your choice!'

Pete Quinn raised his hands. Jonas dismounted and removed Pete's six-gun and strode over to Wally.

'How'd you get on to us?' Wally asked as he was divested of his weapon.

'We followed you out here,' Jonas said.

'Yeah, but so what?'

Marcy said, 'We watched you recover the hidden loot—'

'Damned fool!' Pete snapped.

'I recognized your voice, even though you disguised it for Alfred,' Marcy explained. 'A slight intonation when you used the word "dadblasted". Then I took the writing pad from the telegraph office after you sent your message to Pete here. The impression was plain enough for me to read : "Staying at Falls a few days. Meet at Guthrie on 25th . . ." – which is today.'

'You and that telegram!' growled Pete.

'It might have been an innocent telegram, save it was sent to Pete Quinn. I knew the name from a few wanted dodgers. And this robbery tied in with a few inside jobs on other routes.'

'You've done this before?' Wally wailed.

'Sure,' laughed Quinn, a hint of pride in his voice. 'I usually sucker the shotgun rider to go sick. Or if they're keen, hell, they can do the robbery for me – like you. As long as I get my cut!'

'Who are you?' Wally asked, finally.

Jonas said, 'He's Horace Q. Marcy, an agent of Wells, Fargo.'

EPILOGUE

A GAMBLE

'So,' Saul said, 'Wells, Fargo are going to hang their green shingle on your stage depot?'

'Yes, that's why Smith wanted to buy me out. It should be quite lucrative. If Wells, Fargo stays, our fortunes will be linked with theirs. It can only be good news.'

'I'm pleased for you, Ruth.'

'Will you stay on and work here?'

'That depends. . . .'

'What are you going to do about Erica Beal?'

'I don't rightly know. I like her—'

'Whatever you decide, I'll back you. It's your life. All I will say is, don't live your life alone. Find somebody to share it with. It makes the living a whole lot easier.'

'And will you take your own advice?'

'I'm thinking on it.' She smiled. 'There's a big age difference. And I haven't looked at Jonas in that way before.'

'Give it time, Sis.'

'Yeah, we don't need to rush into anything, do we?'

'There's no rush,' Virginia said as Alfred Boddam tabu-

159

lated the cost of a selection of tools on the counter.

Alfred glanced up and winked. 'Not a gold rush, then?'

'Nope,' smiled Daniel. 'Just cabin rebuilding, that's all.'

'How are you feeling?' Virginia asked Alfred.

He put down his pencil. Kitty Riley was busy stacking boxes of cartridges on a shelf at the other end of the counter. She was smiling as she worked. 'I'm improving every day. I've given up coach driving,' he said. 'I've got this idea and Kitty and Spence are keen I give it a try.'

'What's that?'

'I aim to offer a delivery service to our customers. You never know, it might catch on.'

'Well, I for one would appreciate it,' Daniel said. 'Especially while I'm rebuilding. It can save me a lot of time if you deliver.'

'Gives us more time to "catch-up", honey,' Virginia whispered.

Daniel reddened and grinned. 'Yeah.'

'It's a bit of a gamble,' Alfred admitted.

Virginia gripped Daniel's hand. 'Life's all a gamble, Alfred,' she said. 'But I reckon it's worth taking the risk.'